With thanks to the peoples of Khayelitsha who welcomed me into their homes and who I took into my heart

January - Heidi	1
February - Rosa	25
March – Kerensa	39
April - Susan	53
May – Judith	71
June – Kayla	84
July – Eva	96
August – Charlotte	108
September – Marianne	118
October – Helena	132
November – Michelle	143
December – Sally	154
Another January	164

the first day of each new month brings with it fresh possibilities to dream

January - Heidi

It was just another first day of the month; just another first day of January; just another first day of the year; just another first day of the rest of his life; another chance to leave the past behind.

It was sometimes problematic for Matthew to differentiate between what had just passed and what had yet to come. The delineations between his past, his present and his future held little significance but the lack of clarity and the indeterminate nature of the passage of time gave solace to his otherwise comfortable existence.

His divorce four years ago had been amicable, the settlement had been fair and, with no children to complicate the proceedings it had been mercifully quick. Sally had had an affair with his close friend Simon, but when he found out about her infidelity, he recalled feeling shocked but disconcertingly unhurt. In fact, he had felt more hurt by Simon's actions than Sally's. Matthew had found it possible to retain some sort of friendship with Sally but not so with Simon.

Considering that she had had an affair, he concluded that she could no longer claim to love him and considering he had not felt hurt by the revelation, he concluded that he no longer loved her. He occasionally reflected on the thought that, had he still loved her then, not only would her affair have shattered him, he would have been unable to forgive and a less amicable divorce would have inevitably ensued which would have torn their souls apart. The ultimate conclusion that love no longer bound them offered them both the easy and logical solution of a divorce, of staying friends and to follow their own separate paths.

He and Sally had indeed remained friends of sorts and both he and she had quickly and easily moved on. Or rather, Sally had moved on and moved in with Simon, whilst Matthew had largely stayed still. Matthew had moved on from Sally, but his life stubbornly refused to follow suit. However, this was not a problem for him. He had a steady, secure job lecturing in anthropology at St Michael's College in Cambridge, a comfortable Edwardian terraced house facing Jesus Green and a good circle of friends and acquaintances to fill the void left by his failed relationship with Sally.

Christmas in Reading with his parents and elder sister, Jane, had been boringly predictable but reassuringly comforting and the New Year's Eve party he was just recovering from had been simultaneously both mundane and unavoidable. The only thing worse for him would have not to have been invited. Attending was a chore, but a necessary one. The fact that his long-term friend and admirer, Eva, had chosen him for a kiss at midnight as Big Ben chimed twelve had assuaged his apprehension that he might, yet again, be the only partygoer left alone and self-conscious as the slurred words to *Auld Lang Syne* beckoned in the New Year.

Matthew had easily hidden from himself the fact that the amorous encounter with Eva had happened despite her being in a long-term relationship with her partner, Dave.

Dave had been called away to America on urgent business and was unable to attend the party, leaving Eva to drink herself inexorably towards Matthew. Although grateful of Eva's drunken osculation, he had no reciprocal amative intent for her. In fact, he had no romantic nor amorous intent for any of the women in his circle of friends. Most had attempted some sort of predatory coup on him since his divorce but all had given up apart from Eva. Eva had maintained her coquettish behaviour towards Matthew despite his rebuffs and despite her long-standing relationship with Dave. Matthew was aware of the unrequited love triangle he endured with Eva but felt little responsibility for it and gave it little cerebration. That he had accepted her New Year's embrace and kiss so willingly and gratefully impinged only momentarily on his conscience despite acknowledging her distress as she left the party alone. He wondered if he should have offered to escort her safely to her house given that it lay less than five minutes from his, but he advised himself not to proffer any false expectations.

For Eva, walking home alone was comfortless whilst for Matthew it was a reprieve. Had any thoughts of his callous behaviour still disquieted him as he turned the key to his chicly decorated Cambridge home, they were quickly dispelled as he downed a final dram of single malt whisky before slumping on top of his duvet still half dressed. The ensuing drunken sleep cleansed his conscience but banked the residual alcohol ready to plague his awakening with a stubborn headache and dry palate.

Today was another new day, another new month, another new year and another new start. It wasn't going to be Eva, but somewhere out there he knew a soulmate was waiting to accept and reciprocate the love he would willingly offer and that he so desperately needed. Someone who would complete his life. He was happy to wait. He knew that he would not find the love he sought at a party, at a club or in a new acquaintance's bed. He was happy to wait until circumstance presented him with a suitable partner and even then, he would bide his time.

He and his now ex-wife had met too young and had married too quickly. He had learned the lessons of infatuation and was, he told himself, now mature enough to find and recognise true love when it presented itself to him and when he could return the romantic idolatry. Whilst not actively seeking love he had readied himself for the moment it whispered to him in order for an apposite response to grasp the opportunity.

Matthew's life was filled with voluminous work and a soupcon of leisure. Lectures would begin in two weeks for which he still had to prepare and the field trip he was leading to South Africa was going to occupy a lot of his time both before and after the event. The mountain of work raised up before him blotting out the possibility of diversion to any repose.

Nonetheless, his life was comfortable, secure and predictable which mostly gave his life enough contentment and meaning to satiate his emotional appetite. His existence was that of a happy, middleclass professional enjoying escalating success and looking forward to new and exciting career challenges. Thoughts of the lack of a partner rarely allowed themselves to intrude into his daily, weekly, monthly or yearly routine except on the first day of the first month of each year.

New Year's Day gave him pause for contemplation forcing him to reflect on how, although he had left his past life behind, his new life had doggedly refused to begin. Instead, he was destined to make great professional strides and to enjoy endless achievements doing exactly the same things.

Today was another new beginning but, as usual, one without a plan. Today was another new beginning to another new chapter to an old story. His work, the quintessential middleclass dinner parties and the occasional work trips overseas were enough to fulfil him to a significant enough degree for him not to dwell on the paucity of his eudemonia. For now, his lone walk on Jesus Green was enough to fuel his determination to shed both the alcoholic excesses of the previous night and the romantic temperance of the previous year.

It was still only 9 o'clock in the morning. He had had little sleep but wanted to drink in the crispness of the air together with drinking in the catalyst of caffeine before Cambridge began raising itself from its self-imposed, collective hangover. The unexpected brittleness of the sun following a grey winter seemed to have surprised the plants and shrubs in their manicured beds causing them to blink and look around as the sap-sodden grass teased its intent to emerge from slumber and pave the vista with its generous, lush, green baize.

The early blooming narcissi lazily hung their heads as Matthew ignored their welcoming colours. A handful of dogwalkers and joggers barely intruded into his introspective solitude but the freshness of the cold sun, the rain-washed walkway and icy blue sky subliminally raised both his spirits and his hopes.

This was to be the best year of his life. This was to be the year that the final piece of the jigsaw of his soul would supervene and complete his existence. This was to be the year he would find a companion with whom he would share his journey.

His recent promotion to Head of Faculty had edged him towards a professorship even at the unusually young age of thirty-five, his new book was nearing completion and the master's degree he had been preparing to offer to his most able post-graduate students was ready for scrutiny by his peers before inclusion in the impending recruitment drive. The year ahead was full of challenges, full of potential successes and full of exciting prospects but the year ahead left him deplete.

None of these thoughts intruded into his sobriety deeply enough or for long enough to cause disquietude. This was simply who he was and what he did. Life was good. Life was kind. Nonetheless, Matthew needed coffee before he could begin the rest of his life and the Café Cam would fulfil that immediate requirement.

A short walk was thoughtlessly completed and, as he entered the doorway of the café, the owner, Cameron D'Arcy who had obtained a PhD under Matthew's supervision but had then opted to run a café rather than pursue an academic career, nodded a salutation and began preparing a flat white without the need for a verbal prompt.

Having acquired his coffee, a bench on Jesus Green overlooking the River Cam was routinely located where he once again found himself sitting with thoughts of possibilities and of prospects signposting him into the new year. This was Matthew's bench. This was the bench he always occupied to analyse the world ethereally floating by him as he scrutinised passers-by. It nestled on Jesus Green and gave a comforting aspect of residential river boats sleeping on the River Cam.

The number of dogwalkers and joggers increased in tandem and they were joined by lovers walking in lockstep as slowly as possible in order to prolong the romantic reciprocation that their shared night of drunken passion had bestowed upon them. The quiet, newness of the early morning begrudgingly began giving way to an energetic bustle and Matthew decided it was time to move on away from his solemn detachment and to head back to his mundane reality. He glanced around to locate the litterbin to dispose of his takeaway coffee cup but was immediately interrupted by an agitated mortal clutching a smart phone. Her voice pierced his introspection with its urgency.

"Excuse me, I'm really lost. I'm trying to find the ArtTime Gallery. I'm supposed to be meeting a friend there but I'm really late. I've been following Google Maps on this damn phone but I've been going round in circles for ages."

Matthew lazily raised his eyes to meet the importunateness of hers. He raised his arm to denote the general direction in which she should depart and annotated his gesture with the minimum of words necessary to hasten her removal from his consciousness.

"No problem. You're not far. Just go up that way. Over there to the bridge, then left, left again further down and you'll see it. It's about 5 minutes away, that's all. You can't miss it."

"Oh, thanks, but I swear I've been that way a dozen times already. I'm being so dim. No worries. I'll try again. Sorry to have bothered you."

Sensing her agitation and grasping the opportunity to delay the return to his inevitable corporality, Matthew chose instead to act as her guide.

"Hang on, I'm going in that direction. I'll show you."

Matthew's lie was intended to offer help to a stranger without making her feel awkward or indebted. However, the cold truth was that he was literally and metaphorically going nowhere and so a circuitous route back to his house would be of little consequence.

"Are you sure? I don't want to put you out."

"Sure. Come on, follow me. It's hardly any distance. To be honest, it is easy to miss. You can walk past it without noticing it."

"That's really kind. I'm nearly an hour late. I messaged him to tell him to wait but he didn't reply."

"Your boyfriend?"

"Well, er, this is a bit embarrassing. No, not exactly. Well, er, maybe. I got together with him last night at a party. He wanted me to go back to his place, but I told him that I wasn't like that. So, I said I'd meet up with him for a coffee this morning instead."

"Well, if he is serious, then I'm sure he'll be there. We'll be there in a minute."

Matthew quickened his step both in a display of empathy for his new acquaintance's dilemma but, moreover, to rid himself of her as quickly as possible. He didn't mind acting as a temporary guide but baulked at the level of personal information she was inflicting on him. Whilst he had yet again begun the new year partnerless, he now found himself facilitating a complete stranger in her pursuit of a new and potentially meaningful relationship of her own.

Approaching the ArtTime Gallery brought his new companion cause for audible distress.

"Shit. He's not here. I'm such a dork for thinking he would be."

She began an agitated interrogation of the rendezvous location as though her circumvolution might spirit his body into her presence. Matthew managed to interrupt her meaningless quest in an attempt to seek an escape route from the tragic drama which was inflicting itself on his disinterest.

"I'm sorry."

"No. It's me. The truth is, I've fancied him for ages and I thought I'd finally got a date with him. I'm so dumb."

"I'm sure there is someone out there for you. Don't worry."

Matthew heard the words tumble out of his mouth and cringed at the unbelievable shallowness of the platitudinous ineptitude of his social inability. He reminded himself that, although he was confident in professional circles, he was awkward in social ones.

"Yeah. I keep telling myself that. I just keep chasing the wrong ones – shit, that makes me sound desperate, doesn't it?"

Matthew drew a deep breath and struggled to find another platitude to hide the fact that he agreed with her. The ensuing hiatus caused by his inability to find any words to cover his lack of social competence was immediately taken up by his distressed companion.

"Anyway, thanks. You were very kind. I won't keep you."

"No worries. Good luck."

"Good luck," he thought, *"what the hell am I saying? I really do master in shallowness."*

They simultaneously turned to begin a parting manoeuvre before realising they were now both retracing their steps in concord with one another.

"Oh," she said, "I thought you said this was on your way."

"Yes, you are not wrong, I did say that. I might have lied just a little bit. It just seemed easier to say that rather than say I'll take you to the gallery despite it being in totally the opposite direction I was planning on going."

The brief laughter his confession brought lightened his spirits and temporarily deceived him of the fact that he might have at least a minimum quota of social capital after all.

"I'm Matthew by the way."

"I'm Heidi. Pleased to meet you."

Their conversation was interrupted by bemused smiles which were left suspended in the chasm between them as they approached the bench at which they had met just minutes before. Heidi broke the verbal impasse.

"To be honest, I'm glad he wasn't there. He's a bit of a player actually. It would have been a big mistake. I don't know why I got my hopes up."

"Too much detail again," thought Matthew.

"Anyway, Matthew, thanks again. I think I'll just pick up a coffee and head off home. To be honest I've got a bit of a hangover. Coffee is very much needed."

"No excuses needed, Heidi. I'm feeling just the same. Come on, I need a coffee too. I'll buy you one."

Having just finished a coffee, the lie he just expressed took him by surprise, but before he could begin interrogation of the fact that he had just offered a complete stranger a coffee, Heidi again interjected.

"Great. Except I'm buying. Just to say thank you for taking me to the gallery."

Matthew wanted to decline but his tiredness heralded the pathway to his compliance. Five minutes later after visiting the Café Cam they were seated together on the bench which had been their unintended rendezvous, each clutching takeaway coffee cups as security blankets and both suddenly aware of the lack of conversation which dominated their fledgling relationship.

Matthew took the opportunity to begin a visual analysis and the inevitable assassination of the appearance of the new corporeal being known as Heidi who had become his transitory caffeine-comrade. She was, he thought overwhelmingly plain looking. Her mousy hair was neither straight nor curly and her skin had an awkward pallor to it. She wore an uninspiring, navy-blue duffle coat below which drab brown trousers led his eyes down to a pair of flat, leather shoes which had clearly enjoyed brighter times. An extravagant and shockingly coloured cotton scarf, which was wrapped several times around her neck, seemed to cause her head to sit ethereally on top of her body as though it had become detached. He concluded the visual annihilation of his new companion as his extrospection gave way to introspection and the realisation that he too, was drab and uninspiring in both his looks and his attire. His wiry brown hair had started to submit to greyness; his jacket was that of a caricature college lecturer complete with worn, leather elbow patches; his brown corduroy trousers were tired and baggy and his scuffed shoes struggled to live up to their intended purpose.

Nonetheless, there he was, drinking a coffee he didn't want with a stranger he wanted to escape from. *"Not the greatest start to the year after all,"* he thought. But, before Matthew had a chance to formulate a coherent escape plan Heidi disturbed his detachment.

"Did you know there is a retrospective by Lethabo Kenyetta on at the gallery?"

"Who?"

"Lethabo Kenyetta. He's a British-South African photographer. He has created a photographic journal of his time living in Khayelitsha."

"Do you know Khayelitsha?"

"No, but I know of it. It's a huge township just outside Cape Town. About two and a half a million people live there. He lived with them for a year and photographed the place, the people and their lives."

"Sounds like an interesting exhibition." Matthew spoke with genuine attentiveness. "So, are you an artist or something?"

"Er, no. Actually, I'm a primary school teacher. OK, confession time – I've no idea what I'm talking about. I just boned up on it because I wanted to impress the guy I just got stood up by. He's into all that stuff which is why I suggested meeting there."

Matthew found himself discarding his social awkwardness and embracing his companion's candour with a laugh which began with near authenticity and ended factitiously.

"Seriously though, Heidi. It sounds really interesting. Believe it or not, I've actually been to Khayelitsha and I have a trip to South Africa planned for later in the year. I'll be spending some time in Khayelitsha again, so I think I'll go and have a quick look at the exhibition. Anyway, did you think that the fact that your date was not waiting outside might be because he had actually already gone inside?"

Heidi failed to acknowledge Matthew's revelation that he had been to Khayelitsha and would be visiting again, but instead focused on her immediate emotional angst.

"Shit, no! Christ, I'm such an idiot. So, he might not have stood me up after all. It was me who stood him up!"

"Well, maybe. Look, I think I'm going to have a quick gander at the exhibition, so why not come and see if he's there?"

"OK. Yes. Come on." Heidi's voice had become urgent and commanding as it directed the duo back towards the gallery.

The day had begun, the month had begun, the year had begun and a new acquaintance had begun. Neither Matthew nor Heidi had planned this new beginning, but now it had invited them, they followed their accidental, parallel paths willingly but apprehensively as they urgently retraced their steps to the ArtTime Gallery in order to bind the newness of their circumspective association.

Entering the gallery and being confronted with images of black children playing barefoot on narrow strips of dry, compacted earth between what appeared to be little more than glorified shacks felt otherworldly to Heidi but familiar to

Matthew. He had concealed his wish to share the fact that he not just visited Khayelitsha, but had worked extensively with the indigenous peoples living there and that his recently published academic paper had been an exploration of the interactions of the black Africans, the coloureds and the whites who lived and interacted there. Finding himself unable or unwilling to share the fulness of his thoughts he instead offered a simple introduction.

"Did you know that Khayelitsha translates as *new home*?"

"Wow. That's incredible. I guess it must be a hangover from apartheid."

"Yes. Exactly so. Apartheid officially ended in the early nineties, but racial discrimination and financial segregation live on in a big way. Some people call it *fiscal apartheid*." By *some people*, Matthew had meant *he* had described it as fiscal apartheid in a lecture he had delivered at a conference at the University of Ottawa.

"So, although apartheid has ended, it kind of lives on in Khayelitsha?"

Although simplistic to Matthew he could find no other words to agree nor disagree with Heidi's interpretation of what was unfolding before them on the walls of the gallery. As he tried to formulate some further, meaningful response, Heidi's anxiety broke into his contemplation.

"Wait here a minute. I'm going to see if Phil is here. I'll be back in a mo."

Phil, Matthew supposed, was Heidi's nearly-date. Almost hidden from himself, he found thoughts swirling around his mind allowing him to hope that the unapparent mortal called Phil would not be located. As the previous night's alcohol and the morning's caffeine battled for dominance and before his machinations could settle in his consciousness and disturb him with their significance, he found himself interrogating the body language of Heidi as she returned alone moments later. Firstly, he read despair but quickly superimposed relief.

"No Phil, then?"

"No. No Phil."

Matthew caught a glimpse of Heidi's next sentence which hadn't found courage to expose itself and the shallow platitudes forming in his subconscious cautioned themselves to stay similarly hidden. Nonetheless they found a means of escape with disturbing ease.

"Well, Heidi …. shall we do the exhibition? I'm probably a poor substitute for Phil, but at least I'm here."

"Very tactful, Matthew. But you are indeed here and Phil isn't. I guess he couldn't be bother to wait for me. So, yeah, let's do the exhibition."

Silence took control and their unspoken words spoke volumes as they turned their backs on their mutual conflictions and diverted their attention to an image of a black woman breastfeeding her new-born child. Heidi was gripped by the gaunt face and the emptiness of the woman's darkly haunted eyes and leaned in to read the notes pinned to the wall alongside the portrait. Having read the notes, she swung round to meet Matthew's heavy, saddened gaze with pain in her own.

"Christ, Matthew. She's only fourteen and she was raped by a drunk and this photo was taken just two days after her baby was born. She was all alone in a shack breastfeeding."

Matthew did not know the woman portrayed in front of them, but knew of the story well.

"Yes, sadly alcoholism is all too common in Khayelitsha. Alcohol driven rape is not uncommon and many children suffer from foetal alcohol syndrome too due to alcohol exposure during pregnancy."

"God, that's awful."

Next, they moved to an image of a boy aged eight. He was small for his age and had a confused, almost whimsical look on his face. He clutched an orange and looked sideways to the camera lens. Again, Heidi leaned in to explore the story behind the image of the diminutive boy.

"Matthew, he'd never seen an orange before. He didn't know what it was or what to do with it."

Again, Matthew knew the context well, but he declined to add further analysis. He had so many stories to add to the images hanging on the walls of the gallery but chose to secrete them from his companion rather than to expose his true familiarity of the content of the images.

Photograph after photograph forced Heidi and Matthew to confront their own comfortable existences until they found themselves standing in front of images of two of the Khayelitsha shacks between which was a full-length mirror forcing them to see themselves embedded within the context of one of the poorest cities in the world. First, they looked at their own images looking back at themselves. Even their dowdy, unkempt attire looked somehow extravagant and obscene. Then they allowed their eyes to interrogate each other. They shared no words despite their thoughts finding coalescence.

Heidi wanted to escape the awkwardness the simulacra forced on her but Matthew willed time to evaporate until his next visit when he could engage in this alternative reality. Even then he had to examine his conscience. He had told himself his anthropological research was aimed at raising awareness of the plight of these forgotten, post-apartheid peoples but, as he watched the uncomfortable couple looking back at him, he had to admit to himself that his research was more to do with advancing his career. Furthermore, whenever he recounted his time in Khayelitsha, he allowed his audiences to assume he had lived in a shack sharing the plight of his research subjects. The truth was that his university research grant allowed him to stay in a five-star hotel in Cape Town and from there to make daily trips to the neighbouring township. The truth that he veiled harried his conscience but never allowed him to present an honest account either of himself or to himself.

Matthew and Heidi concluded their tour but paused by the final words written on the wall by the exit.

The total time elapsed in the photographs in this exhibition adds up to less than one hundredth of one second.

Neither could express their full comprehension of this final proclamation.

Returning to the sharp daylight and to the newly awakened Cambridge residents failed to return them to the normality of their lives. Somehow, they both felt the need to find a way to share the thoughts that the images had summoned from deep within their souls. Somehow, they had to construct a continuation of their encounter. Uncharacteristically, it was Matthew who stumbled upon an opportunity to extend their conversation in the hope that Heidi would accept the invitation.

"Have you seen the time, Heidi? It's gone midday. Where did the morning go?"

"Yes, I know! Time has really shot by." Sensing that she and Matthew were about to end their encounter, Heidi quickly grasped an idea to delay the inevitable parting. "But didn't you say you'd been to Khayelitsha and that you are going again?"

"Yes, I'm a lecturer here in Cambridge and its part of my work. I'll be going again later in the year with some students to do some research with them."

"That's amazing. I'm really jealous. Can I join your course?"

"Yes, no problem. Just apply for my master's degree in anthropology and take on a massive student loan."

"Tempting, but I'm afraid I can't abandon all the little six-year-olds I have to teach how to read and write."

"Actually, there's a small school in Khayelitsha which is run as a charity. You could teach there. It's a charitable school and exists to teach children suffering from foetal alcohol syndrome."

"You know, a part of me would love to do something like that, but I'm not sure I've got the balls to give up everything I've got here."

"Well, you never know what the future holds. Maybe you should follow your heart and do it."

"Look Matthew, I'd love to hear more about Khayelitsha if you have time. What say we grab a sandwich and you let me pick your brains?"

"Yeah, sure. There's a sandwich bar not far from here. Come on."

Having discovered the sandwich bar was closed, they found themselves back at the Café Cam sitting at a table in the window and ordering plates of salad and glasses of fresh orange juice. Intimate and willing conversation followed the lead of the freshness of their lunch and, after returning to what now felt like 'their bench', they reluctantly concluded that it was finally time to part company and return to their respective, dull lives. Matthew had found an ease in his companionship with Heidi which had begged him to find a discourse which might allow him to seek acknowledgement of the fact that he was inextricably and irresistibly attracted to her both physically and romantically. He dared to allow a moment in which he convinced himself the attraction was reciprocal.

Desperately, Matthew rejected his innate reticence and grasped the opportunity which he felt was about to desert him.

"Heidi. Please don't feel obliged to say yes, but the fact is, I've really enjoyed chatting with you today. I don't suppose you fancy meeting up some time, do you? Dinner maybe? Or just a drink? Sorry, I'm crap at this. Sorry … I'm not trying to chat you up or anything. Oh, shit. I wish I'd just learn to shut up."

"Well, I don't know. I've had a good time this morning too. Much better than the party last night if I'm honest. The party was rubbish actually. Although I did make a new girly friend. But look. I'm not sure. It feels a bit weird. I don't normally go round picking up blokes on park benches. Even cute ones like you."

Matthew hurriedly banked the word 'cute' for later analysis and continued.

"Yeah. I know. Sorry. Just forget I said anything. I reckon I just spoiled a perfectly good morning."

"No, you haven't. Look, I tell you what. If you are serious, then I'll meet you here at this exact bench in exactly one month. If you turn up, we'll go on a dinner date. If not …. well, if not, then that's that."

"Deal. February the first. Here."

"Deal. In a month then. During my lunch break. OK?"

"Done. I'll be here. I promise."

With the transaction agreed they sealed the contract with an awkward hug, turned away to stride resolutely back to their separate lives to ask themselves whether something of significance might just have happened but content that actualisation of an answer to the question had been postponed rather than rebuffed or dismissed. Both harboured hope but dared not interrogate the prospect that a meaningful relationship might just have found a seed of germination.

February - Rosa

As memories of January began to fade into the routineness that defined her life, Heidi sipped at her glass of red wine circumspectly as an episode of Grey's Anatomy rolled by almost unnoticed on her television screen. The school term had started predictably and her class had remained a mixture of challenging and submissive little humans. The curriculum was uninspiring and, try as she might, her teaching reflected the same routineness and predictability that the teaching resources she was given demanded of her. Graded as an *outstanding teacher*, Heidi felt underwhelmed at the prospect of yet another Ofsted inspection. She knew she would rise to the challenge but also knew the falseness of it. Her daily teaching was always going to surpass the fabricated lessons she would engineer simply to impress an Ofsted inspector who marched to the beat of the Department for Education drum. The tedious and time-consuming inevitability of endless inspections gnawed at and challenged her professionalism, but she would dig deep in order to retain the badge of honour aspired to by the best teachers. Despite the pressure placed on her to seek senior leadership roles, Heidi chose instead, to concentrate her efforts on classroom teaching leaving her with feelings that she had reached a career cul-de-sac. She was at a career dead-end where excellent teaching would be assumed but not rewarded and where less able teachers would find promotion and become her puppeteers.

Matthew's term had similarly begun with predictable inevitability. A new cohort of students feigning enthusiasm had rotated onto his master's module and he had delivered lectures with faux fervour. Individual and group seminars provided some departure from the monotony of the repetitiveness of his disquisition as students fawned over his academic prowess and as he exposed his vanity by spreading his undoubted knowledge and experience to those students who bothered to turn up. The faculty meetings, however, gave him little pleasure. Not because of the vicious point-scoring that inevitably dominated the proceedings but because he was exceptionally good at vicious point scoring. A fact that always sent him back to his modest, homely abode to fill a wine glass with well-seasoned contrition. His new master's course had been scrutinised, mauled and shredded by his peers at the first of these meetings and then passed with no request for any revision.

The one event on the horizon of predictability spreading out before him was the first of February. Written into his calendar and hidden between meetings and lectures was his private writing time. He had ensured that his allocated private writing time would fall on the first of February thereby giving him the freedom to absent himself from the constraints of the college regime and instead sit on that bench on that green and wait for that primary school teacher who had occupied and haunted his waking imaginations since their first meeting.

It was true that Heidi had found her way into his consciousness but he had dismissed any thoughts that she might actually show up to meet with him. So far, he had forbidden any reflection that he might actually want her to show up, so that he now found himself sitting on that bench, flat white in hand, telling himself that he was glad that she hadn't. Believing that he did not want to see her, allowed remission from the disappointment that she had inflicted on him by her absence.

The clearly remembered arrangement had been that they would meet at that bench on that green during her lunch break. Not knowing when lunch breaks in primary schools happened, Matthew had arrived for midday. In fact, he had arrived half an hour before midday and had strolled around before finding a coffee to act as companion as he sat and waited.

The broken February clouds held the warmth of the watery sun at bay and the rain-filled crocuses and snowdrops barely broke the monotony of the seasonal insipidity whilst the ash, beech and oak were already threatening to begin their inexorable rise to leafy pre-eminence. Nature was doing its best to divert Matthew's attention from his malaise, but he disliked this time of year intensely. For him, the year had already begun but had shown no respite from the sameness of the previous year. Early promise of new and more fulfilling ventures had already faded and given way to the dreary continuance of his normality.

It was another first day of another month and little had changed. There was just a path of drudgery in front of him leading to the inevitable meetings, lectures and seminars. The names and faces in his academic lectures and seminars changed by rotation, but the students remained relentlessly the same. Once again, the opportunities he had promised himself that would lead to a new and exciting future had either failed to materialise or he had failed to grasp. Teaching, writing, meaningless visits to the college bar to numb his isolation together with endless verbal fights at faculty meetings offered little inspiration for him. Even the prospect of the university hierarchy considering him for a professorship failed to lift his spirits.

Considering that more coffee might help stimulate his body if not his mind he began gathering his thoughts into a box labelled, *to be dealt with later over a glass of wine,* when his sobriety was abruptly interrupted by a distantly familiar voice.

"Hiya, Matthew. How are you doing?"

Casting his eyes around in order to attach a face to the familiarity of the voice he initially missed an attractive middle-aged woman on a mobility scooter who had parked alongside him as he sat on that bench on that green. Quickly lowering his gaze, he met the eyes of Rosa, who he immediately recognised as his near neighbour. Although living only a few doors away from Matthew, they had conversed infrequently and superficially over the years. Their paths had seldom crossed further than polite nods and passing chats about the weather. They inhabited separate and different worlds just four doors apart.

Matthew quickly scanned his memories for context in order to summon an apposite salutation. He remembered Rosa, her husband and three children living a few doors from him. Then he remembered Rosa on her own. Then he remembered Rosa disappearing for maybe four weeks before reappearing in a wheelchair.

"Rosa! Hey. Yes, doing OK, thanks. You?"

"Well, just look at me. Can you see what's different?"

Not being able to locate a cache of mental images of his erstwhile acquaintance, he had to confess that could not spot the difference.

"Sorry, Rosa. I'm going to plead *blokishness* here. What is it? Hair? New coat? I give up."

"Christ, Matthew! For a smart bloke you are pretty unobservant. No, not girly stuff. My new mobility scooter. The dog's bollocks, don't you think?"

"Oh, wow, yes. Nice wheels, Rosa."

"State of the art technology. It's a class three. Cost a fortune."

"Sounds great. And I see you have a personalised number plate. *ROSA 1.* Very cool."

"Very naff if you ask me. It was a present. My lovely kids bought it for me. They really shouldn't have."

"I'm sure they just wanted you to have the best."

"No, they really shouldn't have bought it for me. I bloody hate it."

Sensing a sudden shift in the conversation from cordial to crabby, Matthew focussed his mental acquisitiveness and feigned interest.

"What? How come?"

"Well, are you sure you want to hear any of this? I warn you I'm not having a good day. If you ask me again, I'll offload both barrels."

Matthew's curiosity overrode his instinct to escape someone else's ill disposition.

"No, seriously. I'm genuinely interested. In fact, Rosa, to my shame, I don't really know why you are riding a mobility scooter at all. I remember you walking around with kids one day and then in a wheelchair the next. I'd like to say I kept my distance so as not to interfere, but in reality, I might be guilty of being so wrapped up in my own life that I didn't do the neighbourly thing and visit you."

"That's OK Matthew. Funny thing is, when it happened, people I thought were my friends deserted me and others I hardly knew suddenly came up trumps. The fact is, you were neither. You were just a neighbour. You had no cause to take me under your wing. So don't guilt-trip yourself."

"Don't we all have a responsibility towards our fellow neighbours?"

"Jesus! Don't go all evangelical on me or I'll speed off at a staggering eight miles per hour."

"Sorry. Look, I'm not in a hurry. So, if you have a minute, fill me in. Time for me to get to know my neighbour. Start at the beginning. You, a husband and three kids. Then what?"

"Me, a husband and three kids. It sounds like another, distant life. A life I would just love now. Yes, you remember well. Me, Colin-the-Cockwobble and three kids."

"OK, cockwobble? Makes me giggle. I think I get it, but just to be sure, what's a cockwobble?"

"Again, not so smart for a college lecturer, Matthew. Cockwobble – a gay – queer – homo – fudge packer. Need I go on?"

"No, I think I got it."

"So, the day my third little baby fled the nest and went off to university, the cockwobbler-in-chief packed his bag and left to go and live with who I now know was his lover, Stuart."

"Bloody hell! What did you do?"

"I did what any self-respecting middle-aged women who had been abandoned would do. I got pissed. I got pissed a lot. When I finally sobered up, I decided to have some sort of midlife crisis. I went on Tinder for a while until I realised that 'looking for a serious relationship' meant 'desperate for a shag with anyone who swipes right'. After Tinder failed me, I decided to relive my teenage years. I bought a Moto Guzzi V7 Special and went joy riding."

"I remember seeing a bike for a bit. What happened to it?"

"Apparently alcohol and powerful motorbikes are not great bedfellows. It ended up in a ditch and I ended up wrapped around a telegraph pole. Hence the wheelchair. Paralysed from the waist down. No-one else was hurt, thank God, but I got myself paralysed."

"Holy shit! I'm so sorry, Rosa."

"Let's make a pact. You don't start using embarrassing platitudes and I'll not have a go at you. What do you think?"

"Deal. I'll do my best, but to be honest, blurting out embarrassing platitudes is my forte."

"So anyway, long story short. I got a grant to make my house sort of easier to use. I pretty much got used to a wheelchair. Then, my darling kids decided I should get my independence back. So, they bought me this monstrosity."

"That was really kind of them – er, wasn't it?"

"Yes. Of course it was. And don't get me wrong. I know they have their lives to lead and I want them to. I don't want them to be fussing over me. But if they thought buying me an expensive toy would help, it turns out they were wrong."

"How come? It looks the business."

"Have you ever tried getting round Cambridge on one of these?"

"Well, no, but a group of students and I did a wheelchair challenge for a day a while back."

"I bet you had great fun. Then you all jumped up and went for a jog or headed to the bar or maybe had a game of lacrosse or whatever it is you college toffs get up to."

"I take your point. Being in a wheelchair for a day is nothing like being stuck in one every day."

"Indeed. Anyway, how did you get on?"

"Apart from blistered hands, I have to confess that it wasn't a great success. Even shops and cafés boasting wheelchair access were really hard. We had to wait for some of them to get ramps before we could go in. And trying to get a dozen wheelchairs into a shop all at the same time just about brought the shop to a standstill. And, of course, there were lots of shops we couldn't get into at all. So, in all honesty, it was a bit crap. And yes, you are right. It was fun for a day but I was really glad to get up and literally walk away when we had done our stint. So, if you are calling me a hypocrite, then *mea culpa*."

"Well, thank you for your honesty, anyway. Yes, lots of places have ticked all the accessibility boxes, but there is a gulf between their rhetoric and my realty. Over the last couple of years, I've got used to it. I've found my limits and I've found the limits of accessing what you would think to be normal."

"Go on. You've got me hooked."

"Well, for example. To get into town in my wheelchair I have to know which buses have wheelchair access and which don't. Sounds simple until you wait for a bus which, when it arrives, just doesn't happen to have the access that it should have. Or it arrives but the wheelchair space is occupied by mums with their buggies. So, all too often, I just don't bother. Then, even if I get to town, the streets are narrow and full of tourists. The shops are cluttered and café tables too close. Like I say, there is a massive divide between what I should be able to do and what is actually possible. Sometimes I actually get into a café and then some kind Samaritan gives me a hand to clear a way for me, or someone gives up a table by the door for me. I know they are being kind and I don't want to sound ungrateful, but frankly, I want to punch them in the head. It just reminds me that I can't go anywhere or do anything and call myself independent."

"Yeah. I get that. But I'm mystified as to why you don't like your mobility scooter. Isn't it better than your wheelchair?"

"You'd think. So, I can shuffle myself onto it and then head into town. Four miles an hour on the pavement which is barely wide enough for me let alone any pedestrians. They get very shirty with me. I often get shouted at. They tell me I should be on the road. Which isn't true. I'm supposed to be able to use either. So, I get onto the road and try that. Now I'm hurtling along at eight miles per hour holding up all the traffic. They get very road raged if they can't pass. I get hooted at and sworn at all the time. They shout out of their windows and tell me to get on the pavement. I can't win. Either way I'm annoying people."

"That's terrible."

"It's more than I can bare. Anyway. I can tootle around the greens OK. I do actually enjoy that. But then I get this far. I get as far as this bench on Jesus Green. Town is just round the corner and I stop. I really, really want to go into town and get a coffee, but the pavements are narrow, the roads are totally inadequate and the place is crammed with students and tourists. You said it was crap in a wheelchair. Well, I can just about get away with that if I can get a bus into town. But this thing is twice as big. I block the pavement and I block the road. Then I can't realistically get into any of the cafés. I know some mobility users can park up and walk a short distance. I can't. I actually am paralysed. People seemed to understand that when I use my wheelchair I am probably paralysed, but just can't see it if I'm on the scooter. They see a scooter as a bit of a luxury for people who can't get around so well."

"Wow. So, it's partly the practical side of it and partly people's perceptions of you?"

"Yes. For me, it's people's perceptions that really stop me. So, here I am. Within striking distance of a coffee and about to head back home as a failure again. Still, eight miles per hour. Pretty impressive, eh, Matthew?"

"I'm getting there, Rosa. I think I'm getting my head round it. Do you have time to talk some more?" Matthew hoped his question did not reveal that Rosa had now become a research project for the next chapter of his book.

"Time is all I have, Matthew. So, if you want to use me as a research project, I'm all yours."

"Was it that obvious?"

"I'm afraid so. But it'll cost you."

"No worries. I'll grab a couple of coffees from Café Cam and then maybe we could head down to that bench over there just along the Cam a bit and continue our chat."

"Actually, it wasn't a coffee I was begging for. But thank you. I'll accept the coffee. No, I want to pick your brains. The truth is, I'm thinking of applying for your anthropology course. I just wanted to ask you about wheelchair access around your college."

"Oh. Oh, right. Yes. I'll just have to think. Tell you what, I'll grab the coffees and I'll meet you down there by the water."

"Really? Take a look, Matthew. What do you see?"

"Er. Oh, yes. I see a metal width restriction at the entrance to the riverside walk. To stop cyclists, I guess."

"Yup. And which stops me. Don't worry. There is another way. It's right round the other side of those buildings. You get the coffees and I'll go and run over a few tourists. I'll see you down there in about ten minutes. You'll probably be there with the coffees by the time I have taken the scenic route through town. I'll have to go best part of a mile just to travel twenty yards to the riverside over there."

"Another sobering point for me, Rosa. Anyway, I'll get some sushi and stuff too. Let's make a day of it. Let's pick each other's brains to bits. A bit of neighbourly mutuality."

"I'd really like that. I'm finally reaching a point of acceptance about my paralysis and I want to make something of my life. Going back to university might do that. I'll be your research project if you give me the low down on life at college in a wheelchair."

"Perfect. Applications are due in in a month for the next intake for my course. So, this is very timely. See you in a minute."

"Make that fifteen, Matthew."

Reconvening at their chosen rendezvous Matthew was laden with coffee, sushi and sashimi. As he unpacked his culinary stash Rosa was able to direct the conversation.

"Well, Matthew, I did a sociology degree back in the day. Then went into teaching. I reckon I might have a master's in me and it's your anthropology course that grabbed my attention. If I could get my master's, then maybe I'd find some work lecturing or something. Maybe do a doctorate too once I'm on staff. What do you think? Maybe it's a fantasy, but being paralysed has made me re-evaluate my life. My legs have given up but my brain still seems to be working. Which, by the way, is something else people don't get. All too often I'm treated like I must be simple just because I'm in a wheelchair. Some people actually shout at me and use simple language like they think I'm stupid or something. I want to tell them it is them that's being stupid, not me. But of course, I just suck it up and try to accept their intended kindness."

"I think you have a great plan. There's no reason why you can't do a master's and then progress from there. What's more, I'll help. I was thinking. How about you come to college for a day as my guest. Shadow me. Then we'll see for real what it is like in a wheelchair. That would give me loads of ammunition to get things improved. What do you think?"

"You want me to be a human guinea pig?" Rosa paused long enough to witness Matthew's discomfort. "Cool, I'd like that."

"Phew. I thought I'd just gone all patronising again."

"No, I'm messing with you. I'd love a day at your college. I think it would boost my confidence. To be honest, going back to university is a bit daunting. Going back to university in a wheelchair is terrifying."

"Great let's do it. We'll set a date. I won't warn college. It'll be a real test of what is and isn't possible. A real test of access to academic study in Cambridge. I'll go about my usual business and let's see if you can literally keep up. Then you can do your application. There'll be an interview of course and then you can start. My study method is blended – home study and face-to-face seminars. A few lectures on campus too. Hopefully, that will suit you."

"I'm so glad I bumped into you today, Matthew. You are not so bad after all. I'm feeling much more positive now. And don't worry about using me as your research project. I'm up for that too. I reckon I can inject a bit of reality into your academic ivory tower."

Matthew and Rosa continued their verbal ambulation throughout the afternoon before heading home, with Matthew trotting alongside Rosa's speedy mobility scooter, where Matthew began the next chapter of his book.

The accessibility divide: perceptions and realities of access to academic study at UK institutions

March – Kerensa

Another month had lapsed without any opportunity for Matthew to deflect from the demands placed upon him by his role as a Cambridge don. Lectures, seminars and faculty meetings led him to another writing day which again placed him contemplatively on that bench on that green on the first day of another month. His life was full and professionally fulfilling but he was still alone despite being surrounded by students, colleagues, friends and acquaintances.

February had been kind to Matthew. His book had progressed at a pace thanks to the chance encounter with Rosa and his planning for the field trip to South Africa had fallen into place. Not only would the field trip provide a much-needed hiatus to the unstimulating routine of academic life at St Michael's College, it would allow him to reacquaint himself with friends and colleagues at the University of Cape Town who were hosting his visit. In particular he would reacquaint himself with his counterpart Charlotte, with whom he had found a romantic and amorous union when he last visited two years ago.

As he sat on that bench on that green on the first day of March, he tried to reconcile the rhetoric he conveyed of his time in Khayelitsha with its reality. He invariably described himself as having lived and worked with the residents of the township whilst the actuality was that he had resided in a five-star hotel whilst enjoying a carnal dalliance with Charlotte. It saddened him to think that his love life now relied on thoughts of a sexual reunion with a colleague on the other side of the world later in the year after a two-year gap during which the only communication had involved planning his next field trip. That Charlotte was due to join him in Cambridge at the beginning of August in order to help prepare his students for the forthcoming field trip raised his spirits until he began imagining the awkwardness it might bring.

March had brought clear skies and icy gusts from Siberia nicknamed 'The Beast from the East' and, as Matthew sat contemplating where he might direct his life, he was unaware of the attempts being made by the primroses, hellebores and pulsatilla to quelle his feelings of abjection. Even the majesty of the weeping willow, now fully verdant and gently lavishing the banks of the River Cam, failed to penetrate his temporal malaise.

As his spirits began to spiral down like dishwater draining out of a sink, he was joined by a young lady carrying a baby strapped to her chest with an indigo coloured, hemp wrap. Her sandals and her Aladdin pants defined her in Matthew's mind despite the endless assertions in his research methodologies lectures that it is most important to understand your own prejudices and to look beyond first impressions and to accept a research subject on its own merit as it presents itself. He quickly reminded himself that this stranger was not a subject in a participative, interpretive research project but his scrutiny claimed victory as he stereotyped her as a quasi-hippie and a feminist.

He and she nodded acceptance that they were about to share space on the bench and she began unwinding the indigo wrap to reveal a child of approximately two months of age and clearly of mixed-race. Matthew smiled the obligatory smile to acknowledge that he found her progeny to be 'cute' and to obscure the subjective analysis he was inflicting on her. No words needed to be spoken as they danced the silent ballet that strangers engage in when encroaching on each other's privacy in a public space.

Following the unveiling of the infant came the unveiling of her fulsome right breast which was then anointed with something which took on a lilac sheen and which Matthew assumed must be some sort of antibacterial cleanser. He momentarily forgot that he was not invisible and found himself inspecting the spectacle as it literally exposed itself as if he were an audience member in a theatrical production.

"Do you mind?" came the terce interrogation from the lady. Matthew drew back instantly and apologetically.

"Sorry," came Matthew's reflexly contrite response as he realised that he had been crossing an invisible line by scrutinising a stranger's naked breast.

"No, I mean do you mind if I breast feed?"

"Oh, no, of course not. It's the most natural thing in the world."

"Great. I'm a *Foo Warrior*. So, I was going to do it anyway. I just thought I'd ask since you were staring at my breast."

The stranger's words threw Matthew's composure into disarray both because it felt adversarial and because he had no idea what she was talking about.

"Sorry, a what?"

"A Foo *Warrior*. *Foo*, flop-one-out. I think breast feeding is something that should be seen all the time. Don't you agree? It's only a breast, after all. There's a lot of them about. Most women and quite a few men have them, you know."

In fact, Matthew did agree, but this felt like a challenge and his instinct was to retort. Even as the words left his mouth, he knew that it would be a mistake.

"Well, yes, of course. As long as it's discrete."

"Ah, I see. You are one of those, aren't you? By discrete, I assume you mean that breast feeding is OK as long as it can't actually be seen. So, basically, *I'm* OK as long as *I* can't actually be seen. As long as it doesn't make you feel awkward or horny or whatever it does to you. So, what you are saying is that you believe breast feeding should be allowed in public as long as no-one can actually see it? Can't you see how stupid and hypocritical that sounds?"

Matthew knew that his multiple academic degrees would be of no value against what he now knew to be a *Foo Warrior*.

"No, well, er, that's not what I meant."

"Really? Because it is exactly what you said. Are you always in the habit of not saying what you mean or not meaning what you say?"

"Sorry. You are right. I apologise. OK, cards on the table. I really do think breast feeding is OK. OK anywhere, anytime. It's just natural. Actually, it's beautiful. But you were sitting there with your breast hanging out and painted purple talking about being a *Foo Warrior*. I was just a little thrown."

"OK. Sorry. You are forgiven. I guess I do come over a bit strong sometimes. I'm Kerensa by the way. Shall we start again?"

"I'm Matthew. Kerensa is a nice name. Cornish, isn't it?"

"Yeah. It means *love*."

"Beautiful name and beautiful meaning. Matthew is meant to mean *gift of God*."

Matthew now found himself bereft of words to form into any sort of sentence as he continued to watch Kerensa's right breast now with an infant latched on to her erect nipple.

"Do you have children, Matthew?"

"No, but I'd love to have some one day. Just haven't met the right partner yet."

"Well, if you were a woman, you only need a partner for one night if you want to have a baby. To be honest, you only need a partner for about five minutes and even then, you actually only need one microscopic sperm."

Matthew's mind now scrambled for some sort of interesting and meaningful response but instead he resorted to his academic, analytic comfort zone which, once started, was difficult to stop despite him telling himself of the imperative to do so.

"That's a really interesting point, Kerensa. So, what you are saying is that a woman only needs a man for insemination whilst a man needs a woman to accept insemination and then to carry the child. I guess my interrogation of that would be in the woman's case, where she had become voluntarily inseminated what right might the semen donor have over the ownership of the child and in the case of a man inseminating a woman in order to carry his child, what rights would the woman have over ownership of the child?"

As his words cascaded into the space which had become increasingly frozen by the incredulous stare of his new companion, he knew he was digging a large hole, filling it with rancid water and throwing himself in it without a life jacket. His propositions might bear merit as a provocative statement in an academic seminar but sat on that bench on that green with a *Foo Warrior* it would inevitably end badly. Matthew was quick to learn why the term *Warrior* had been attached to the expression *flop-one-out*.

"Jesus Christ, Matthew. Can you hear yourself? *Ownership of a child!* Are you serious? *Ownership of a child!* We do not own each other. Parents do not *own* their children. We do not need to be in a loving relationship with a partner in order to be in a loving relationship with our children. What century are you from? As it happens, I'm in a loving relationship with my son and I conceived him through sperm donation. And yes, before you ask, the sperm wasn't donated by an anonymous donor in an anonymous clinic, it was donated by a friend via his penis inside my vagina. Are you OK with that, then? Natural insemination not unnatural insemination."

Matthew desperately needed to find words to diffuse the attack he was now justifiably being subjected to. Either that, or he desperately needed to get away. He could summon neither. Instead, he ignored the advice he was screaming to himself in his head and began to dig deeper.

"Well, I agree on one level, but I'm not sure, in societal terms, it is as simple as that."

"Ah, that is where you are wrong. It really is as simple as that unless people like you want to make it more complicated. Unless people like you want to be judgmental and judge others by their own narrow prejudices. Why can't you accept other people living their lives differently to you and with a different set of norms and values?"

Matthew took a deep breath and gathered what little was left of his now fragmented rational mind as Keresna removed her child from one breast, exposed the other, painted it lilac and resumed feeding.

"Can we start again? I actually agree with you. I honestly do. I'm a lecturer in anthropology here and I was trying to formulate a provocative statement as though I was in one of my seminars. It came out all wrong. I'm totally ashamed of myself and I'm really sorry. I'm an absolute idiot and I'm sorry."

"OK. Then I'm sorry too. I don't even know you and I had a real go at you."

"You don't need to apologise. You were right and I was wrong. I behaved like a total tit. Oh shit, did I just say tit? I didn't mean tit, I meant idiot."

"I'd stop talking there if I were you, Matthew. If you dig any deeper, you'll disappear up your own black hole. Actually, it is me that needs to apologise to you. I lied to you a little bit to make a point. The truth is that I had a boyfriend and we were in a loving relationship. When I got pregnant, he ran off like I had turned into a lump of kryptonite. To be fair, he made an effort for a while, but he was gone in a month. Now I'm a single mum. I had no right nor reason to lie to you and shouldn't have had a go at you. I'm really sorry. It is true that he donated just one sperm, but it was actually done in an act of love, not as a cold-blooded sperm donation."

"We are a couple of idiots then, aren't we? Albeit that I'm the bigger idiot by a very long mile. By-the-way, I'd never heard the expression *Foo warrior* before. *Flop-one-out* really does express a whole load of interesting stuff. God, I wish I could have you in one of my seminars. I reckon you'd teach my students more in half an hour that I could in a whole term. Actually, you could teach me a whole load of stuff."

"Truce then?"

"Truce. And to prove it, let me buy you lunch. How about some sushi or something down by the river? Well, sorry, I'm making assumptions again. Maybe you just want to get away from me. Frankly, if I were you, I'd take the runaway option rather than the sushi option."

"No, that sounds lovely. If you are sure. Don't feel you have to. I can look after myself."

"I've absolutely no doubt you can look after yourself. I wasn't trying to be patronising or trying to chat you up or anything. You carry on feeding ... er."

"Zak. His name is Zak and he would be very happy to take you up on your offer of a picnic."

"You carry on feeding Zak, and I'll pick up some sushi from Café Cam. I'll be back in a moment. Coffee as well?"

"Can I have a Pukka Peace tea? And I'm vegan too, so can I have vegetable sushi?"

Stifling his amusement at the caricature of herself that she had just sketched he responded calmly before regretting his words.

"Sure, no problem. I'll have the same."

Having purchased the vegan option and spurned the coffee he desired in favour of flavoured water, Matthew returned to rendezvous with Kerensa complete with sushi and teas. He noted that both her breasts were packed away and that she appeared ready to strap her infant to her chest.

"Ready when you are, Kerensa."

"OK, just a minute, I just need to get myself sorted out. Here, hold Zak for a second."

Matthew now found sushi and teas replaced by Zak whilst Kerenza packed baby wipes and a myriad of other baby related items into her backpack.

"Sorry about this, Matthew, I'm like a travelling circus."

Suddenly, and to Matthew's relief, the *Foo warrior* appeared vulnerable and in need of company and support.

"No problem. Tell you what, we are only going a couple of hundred yards. Why don't you grab the sushi and teas and I'll carry Zak? He seems very comfy over my shoulder."

"That would be great. Just remember that I've just fed him."

"Yes, I know. How could I forget?"

"Hum. I don't think you understand. I've just fed him. He'll probably puke on your shoulder in a minute. Just one of the joys of motherhood."

"*Parenthood*, I think you mean. Shit, I've done it again, haven't I? I really am one big patronising git."

"Hah. No. I agree with you on that one. *Parenthood*."

As if to prove the point his mother had made, Zak obediently propelled a stream of regurgitated breast milk onto Matthew's jacket.

"Oh. Yes. I see. Look, let's go and camp up by the river over there and I'll get cleaned up."

"Sorry."

"No problem. All natural. I don't mind. Really."

With a suitable venue agreed upon Kerensa, Matthew and Zak settled, cleaned up breast milk and began sharing sushi along with a less hostile and confrontational conversation.

"So, Kerensa, are you from round here?"

"Yes, I live in a bedsit in the less posh end of the worst road in Cambridge. You?"

"I'd like to lie at this point to offer some solidarity, but the truth is that I've got a nice house just over there with views over the river and I've also got rooms in St Michael's College."

"You don't have to be apologetic. Life just dealt us different cards. Believe it or not I have a Cambridge degree in English Literature. I got a first-class honours from King's. My boyfriend was on a fine arts course there too. It's where we met. I ended up with a degree and a baby bump and he ended up with a degree and gone."

"So, do you use your degree?"

"I tried to, but getting a job with an English degree and a very obvious baby bump didn't go well. I guess they thought I'd be there for five minutes and then ask for maternity leave. I can't blame them I suppose. It's not really something a man ever has to deal with. So, it left me feeling rather victimised and angry. I ended up prioritising Zak rather than getting a job. There was actually no other choice. I'm now a single mum on benefits wondering how to get my life back together after my boyfriend ran off to enjoy his life leaving me to pick up the pieces of my life on my own."

"And I'm a single man with a good job, more than enough money and loads of privileges. I totally respect you for what you are doing and I hope you don't resent me for what I am."

"Don't be stupid. Of course I don't resent you. I'm sure you deserve what you've got. I'm going to have to get through this first and then look for better times. I don't really have a plan but all I know is that it will include Zak. If I ever find myself feeling sorry for myself, I just look at Zak and realise how lucky I am."

"You might not believe this, and I hope it doesn't sound patronising again, but I'm actually a bit jealous of you. Despite all that I have, my life is a bit empty. I think I need a Zak in my life."

"Seriously? Well, all I can say is that I like the sounds of what you've got, but I wouldn't trade with you. I'd choose Zak every time."

"Yes, I get that. We really do illustrate the different way society treats different genders, don't we? Erm, don't read too much into this, Kerensa. I'd really like to carry on this conversation, but I've got to go. I've got a tutorial with a student in a bit. I don't suppose you and Zak would like to join me for dinner or something later, would you?"

"That's very kind, but we are on different paths in different worlds. I think that's how it is going to be. Funny, isn't it? What a very different journey a single sperm can send you on."

"OK. I understand. I promise I wasn't chatting you up and I definitely wasn't being patronising. I really enjoyed talking to you about your path and your place. But no worries. I wonder if our paths will converge again one day. I genuinely hope so." Matthew tried to remove from his mind the notion that Kerensa had just become a longitudinal research study with potential for a chapter in his book. "Well, I guess I may see you around then."

"Yes. I'm often on this green. If I see you, I'll make a point of saying hi. And I promise not to have a go at you next time. To be honest, Matthew, considering that you are such a pratt you are not so bad. The fact is, sometimes my life feels tough and today hadn't been a good day. I've been up all night with Zak and then a load of bills arrived in the post. I came to the green to get away and clear my head. I think you might just have accidentally found yourself in my firing line. But thanks for lunch and thanks for putting up with me."

"Don't worry about it. Did you know that pratt is slang for buttocks?"

"Yes, I'm an English graduate, remember. But you're proving yourself to be a pratt again, if you don't mind me saying."

"Once again, Kerensa, you are absolutely right. But seriously. I hope we hook up again some time. I've really enjoyed our little encounter - and Zak, vomit and all, is adorable."

"Sure, me too."

With a nod and a smile, Matthew collected their rubbish together and left as his thoughts were aligning themselves into sentences and paragraphs before the familiarity of his darker thoughts had the opportunity to cloud his perception. He became preoccupied with thoughts of another chance encounter with another interesting lady but which had again led to nothing more than an academic treatise.

Later that day as he recalled the chance events on the green, his mind kicked into gear, his fingers rattled on the keyboard of his laptop and another chapter of his book took shape.

Parenthood as a Moral Imperative: Stigmatisations and implications of voluntarily insemination

April - Susan

April brought with it some respite from the relentless academic rigours placed on Matthew by his superiors who encouraged him to emulate their Cambridge professorial personas. In reality, although there was respite from lecturing, April would be filled with writing and preparation which gave continuance to the inescapable, professional journey he was travelling.

Once more, with flat white in hand, finding that bench on that green, Matthew took in the optimism of the April air and allowed the kaleidoscopic colours of the tulips and anemones to momentarily distract him from thoughts of Heidi which had followed him since their chance encounter three months ago. Despite Heidi not having re-entered his life as planned on the first day of February, he had irrationally retained a residual hope that she may yet find her way to *that bench*. At the very least, being on that bench gave succour to his latent fantasy.

The minutes had passed awkwardly after he had emptied his coffee cup and he made a conscious effort to not look left and right in the hope that a Heidi-shaped figure may drift into view and back into his life. As his watch showed one o'clock, his disappointment gained traction and he began formulating excuses for his stupidity. Another thirty minutes lapsed and, as he began to force his departure, a non-Heidi-shaped being sat down adjacent to him and threw him what appeared to be a consolatory half smile as though she had read his emotional discomfort. His forced smile reciprocated hers as involuntary words slipped, ill-formed, out of his mouth and reluctantly clawed their way through the vacant space between them.

"No offence, but I'm off now."

Once more, Matthew cringed at his social ineptitude.

"None taken," was the trite but better formed response.

"Sorry. I have a tendency to say stupid things to complete strangers."

"No worries. Actually, now we are best friends can I ask where you got your coffee from? I'm just visiting Cambridge and really need a sit down with some caffeine. I'm just off a long-haul flight."

Relieved at the stranger's apparent acceptance of his conversational inability, he continued.

"Yeah. There's a café just along the road. I'll show you. I was just going to get another one anyway."

"Really? That would be great. I'm Susan, by the way."

"I'm Matthew. Nice to meet you. You say you are just visiting? Where from? You sound American."

"No. Canadian. You should never mix the two up. We Canucks are the ones *with* healthcare and *without* guns."

"Canucks?"

"Slang for Canadians."

"Shit. So sorry. I lecture in anthropology here. You'd think I might be smart enough to tell a Canadian from an American."

"Don't worry. It happens all the time. You Brits always make that mistake. You are forgiven. Just don't do it again."

"OK. Let's start again. So, you are Canadian. Which part?"

"Ottawa. Do you know it?"

"Yeah, a bit. I delivered a paper at a conference there a couple of years ago. It's a very cool city. Although, I didn't have much time to look around. Are you just on holiday or are you working?"

"Working. I'm actually doing a guest lecture here. I lecture in Social Studies and Humanities at the University of Ottawa. I'm delivering my paper here tomorrow."

"Oh, wow. No way. Which College?"

"King's. Is that where you lecture? Maybe you are coming to my presentation?"

"No, I'm at St Michael's."

"Right, so I guess you won't be at my presentation then."

"Nope. King's and St Michael's are arch enemies. You'd think we academics would collaborate, wouldn't you, but we keep our faculties strictly to ourselves. Point scoring and competition is what drives us I'm ashamed to say."

"You forget, I'm in the same business. I'm not at all surprised. Small world though."

"Yeah. Cambridge is a very small world."

"Anyway, so, you are a Cambridge don? Do you do the whole punting thing too? I was hoping to give it a go whilst I'm here."

"Er, well, yes. I'm a diva at punting."

"Actually, I think that is a *divo* at punting. Unless you are secretly a woman."

"I stand corrected. Anyway, since we are fellow academics and, broadly speaking working in the same field, what say we grab that coffee and then I'll treat you to an expedition along The Backs in one of St Michael's private punts. It's one of the perks of being a lecturer here. I get to walk across the college grass and then use their punts."

"Is that true? That only dons can walk on the grass and students can only do so if accompanied by a don? I thought that was just made up."

"Yes, I'm afraid it is. Stupid, eh? So, what do you think? Coffee, walk on a bit of grass and then a punt along The Backs? We can call it international collaboration between the University of Cambridge and The University of Ottawa since, strictly speaking, we are both working."

"You're on. Maybe I could bore you with some of the bits of my presentation. I'd love to get your feedback."

"Sounds like a plan. Let's go."

Heidi, or rather the absence of Heidi, was dismissed from thought and Matthew embraced the opportunity to engage the time of a visiting lecturer and to show off his academic territory.

Coffees were duly purchased from the Café Cam and Matthew led the way through Cambridge announcing the name of each college they passed despite Susan being able to read the signs outside each one which boasted their inclusion in one of the world's most prestigious universities. Finally arriving at St Michael's College, Matthew nodded a cursory acknowledgment in the direction of the porter and Susan stifled a bemused smile as she soaked in the image of a diminutive man complete with a small moustache, a watch fob and a bowler hat.

"Hi, James. She's with me. She's guest lecturing at King's. I'm just going to go over her paper with her. Can you sign her in?"

"Sir. Madam." James doffed in deference to the presence of the two academics. "If you wouldn't mind autographing this, Madam."

James offered Susan a clipboard with a visitor proforma attached and opened the heavy, wooden door to allow them access to the hallowed grounds. Passing through the archaic, metal studded portal felt to Susan like passing through a gateway to a time which only existed in the period movies she was addicted to and into a world alien to the relative modernity of her own university.

"Wow, it's just like in the movies I've seen. So, are we?"

"Are we what?"

"The grass! I want to walk on the grass. In my university grass is common land. Students do everything short of fornicate on it. Come to think of it, there is a bit of fornication on the grass too, especially during the summer ball. It is so different here."

"Oh, that." Matthew summoned false modesty in his voice as his pride began to rise like spring sap. "Yes, of course, follow me. Strictly no fornicating, but you can walk on the grass with me."

Matthew led the way diagonally across the immaculately laundered quadrangle at an overly lackadaisical pace to emphasise that he was a don and therefore must been seen contemplating erudite propositions with a fellow academic from overseas. Susan followed half a pace behind and swivelled her head to make sure that this moment in time was being captured in the memories of the lesser mortal undergraduates who were forced to walk around the perimeter of the baize turf.

"Do you live here, Matthew?"

"Here on campus? No. I do have rooms here but I only use them for study. I have a house about twenty minutes away. Tell you what, if you are serious about going over your paper, then we could go up to my rooms after we've been punting."

"Perfect. Thank you so much."

"No worries."

Matthew led the way though narrow, dark, musty corridors emerging onto another, less well manicured lawn beyond which lay The Backs. He explained that The Backs referred to a stretch of the River Cam which ran along the back of some of the major colleges in Cambridge including St Michael's. Susan concealed the fact that she knew this in order to allow Matthew his ongoing, ill-concealed immodesty.

Having selected a punt pole, he stepped into a punt with the name *Flora Belle* inscribed in flamboyant, gold calligraphy on the side. He steadied the float and extended a hand to assist his new comrade as she followed him and found a seat.

"First question, Matthew. What's the punt pole called?"

"Good question. It's got a technical name. It's called a *punt pole*." His well-rehearsed attempt at humour allowed him to offer Susan a warm and inclusive smile.

"Really?"

"Really. I think it is called a *quant* in Oxford, but we aren't so posh here. We just call it a *punt pole*."

"OK. Not hard to remember, then."

"And here's some more useless information for you to feed back to your faculty when you go home. The flat bit I'm about to stand on is called the *till*. I'll be standing on it and punting from the back so we can face each other and have erudite conversations inspired by the amazing architecture and dreaming spires of the colleges as they float by. They do it the other way round in Oxford so we say they are all stupid there because they can only punt backwards."

"Yeah, I heard there is no love lost between Oxford and Cambridge. What's next?"

"You sit there and relax. I've just got to get my shoes off then we can be on our way. I'll give you a quick tour of The Backs and then you can have a go if you like."

"Great. I can't believe I'm doing this. It's been on my bucket list for years."

Matthew's pride propelled him barefoot to the flat till at the rear of the punt before he placed the punt pole on the bank and gently pushed them out into the still waters of The Backs.

"Always bare feet, Susan. You can spot the pros from the tourists. They always keep their shoes on. Anyway, it is really simple. Punt pole into the water. Give a good push followed by a good twist to stop it digging in and yanking you off. Then let it drag for a bit to keep your course steady. Simple. You'll get it in no time."

Matthew continued his punting masterclass whilst superscribing a narrative announcing the name of each college in turn as they drifted by. He expertly avoided tourists as they lost control of both their hired punts and then their footing before plunging into the icy water. He bristled with pride as he escorted his charge under the Bridge of Sighs conscious of a panoply of visitors to Cambridge capturing their voyage on their smart phones.

Having completed his tour-cum-punting-lesson and turning the punt through one hundred and eighty degrees to redirect it back St Michael's College, he offered Susan the opportunity to take charge. With some degree of wobble and hesitancy, she removed her shoes as instructed and mounted the till ready to show her prowess with the punt pole. Her immediate command of punting technique allowed Matthew time to pause and to indulge in the inevitable attempted assassination of his new companion's appearance. He had admitted to himself early in life that this practice enabled him to avoid further progression of any flirtatious behaviour that might be inflicted on him or which he might be tempted to inflict on a female companion. Avoiding flirtatious overtones avoided any chance of what he considered would be the inevitable rebuff and disappointment. Finding fault allowed him to find distance and establishing distance protected the fragility of his self-confidence which was hidden behind the brash academic persona which he had cultivated.

To his dismay, he found himself admiring his new punting tutee and fellow academic. Her wild, blonde hair described a carefree, even dangerous spirit reinforced by a rainbow-coloured jumper and baggy, cotton trousers. This was someone who was confident enough about her body to adorn it with and hide it behind careless and flamboyant attire. Her face conveyed a contentment and happiness that Matthew found himself wanting to share. Try as he might, he could find no fault and instead was drawn to her with disturbing ease.

Whilst not wanting to end the scrutiny of what to him had become an exquisite comeliness he conspired to hijack her to share cerebral exchanges in this rooms.

Finally retaking control of the punt to usher it back onto its private mooring he then took his consort back across the college's quadrangle of grass and into the stone building which was steeped in enigmatic history, up the worn, polished wooden staircase and to the door proudly adorned with the portent, *Dr Matthew Huxley*. He pushed the door firmly to demonstrate his command over the portal and led Susan into the malodorous, oak panelled room. Matthew abhorred smoking, but the wooden panels had absorbed the odour of generations of pipe and cigarette smokers bestowing an egregious and almost claustrophobic atmosphere.

"Grab a seat. Tea?"

"Oh, God, that is so English. If you sit down, you have to drink tea. Yes, thank you kindly Doctor Huxley. I think *milk, no sugar* is the correct response."

"Exactly so. I see you have made yourself at home already."

Tea and biscuits were conjured and discourse flowed effortlessly as the two academics duelled over the finer points of the paper that Sally was due to deliver the following day at King's College.

"Don't laugh, Matthew, but my paper is about the United Nations Universal Declaration of Human Rights …"

"Er, no, not a laughing matter."

"No, you interrupted …"

"Sorry. I'll keep quiet."

"It's about the Universal Declaration of Human Rights compared and contrasted to Facebook's Community Standards."

"Ah. Clever. I see where that's going. You are doing an imaginative take on the UDHR in the context of social media. I'm genuinely impressed. I'm always trying to come up with modern contexts for old concepts to try to engage my students. I pretty much consistently fail in that pursuit. Looks like you've nailed it."

"Phew, you got it. I was a bit worried it might be a bit too far out there."

"No. Brilliant. Go on."

"OK. So, I go through the articles. You know, Articles 1-2: Basic Rights. Articles 3-12: Personal Rights. Articles 13-17: Political Rights. Articles 18-21: Freedom of Thought. Articles 22-27: Economic and Social Rights. Articles 28-30: Duties to the Community. But then I place the Facebook Community Standards alongside. I start with Facebook's Commitment to Voice: Authenticity, Safety, Privacy and Dignity. Then the Community Standards themselves: violence and criminal behaviour, safety, objectional content, integrity and authenticity and respecting intellectual property. There's astonishing overlaps in the content albeit expressed in different contexts."

"Wow. Seriously impressive. But what about the applications of the UDHR and Facebook Standards? I guess they are both global in their own contexts."

"Indeed. You are miles ahead already. Lots of fine words, but trying to establish criteria for measurement is a bit of a nightmare."

"Sad, isn't it. We are so good at lining words up to look good but then they just stay on the page."

"Well, it's more complicated than that. It depends where you stand as to whether the freedoms and protections are effective or not. Then it gets even harder because I have a stab at international comparisons of the application of the UDHR and Facebook Community Standards comparing wealthy capitalist states with developing countries and democracies with authoritarian regimes."

"Oh, Susan, I am so jealous. I wish I had come up with that. And what did you find?"

"Matthew, I'm shocked. I think we both know that good research never gives answers, it only poses better questions."

"Again, I stand corrected."

"Did you know there are over two billion people signed up to Facebook? And can you remember when the UDHR was published?"

"Wow! Two billion! That's incredible. No, I knew there were lots of people on Facebook, including me, but two billion! As for the UDHR – er – I guess it was published in the late fifties. After the war."

"Tenth of December 1948. What's more, it paved the way for more than seventy human rights treaties."

"Including Facebook Standards?"

"Well, maybe, but it's fun to play with the idea. At least I got a provocative paper out of it. To be honest I don't come to any conclusions. I leave it to the reader to come to their own conclusions and hopefully provoke them to grapple with their own prejudices."

"OK, so, like, does freedom of speech include the right to preach hatred or to incite people to violence? I love it. I just love it. So, you are comparing the UDHR with Facebook Standards and inviting your audience to confront their own prejudices and to raise important questions. The perfect academic paper. Brilliant!"

"Exactly that. Great for seminars. But I also reckon I could muster up a research grant to take it further. So, my presentation tomorrow is also a kind of pitch to see if King's will take the bait and offer me a research fellowship. I'd just love to have a year in Cambridge."

Matthew spent a brief moment agreeing that it would be wonderful if she could spend a year in Cambridge. Especially if it meant a year in Cambridge with him. Collecting realism together he dispelled his wishful thoughts and continued.

"I am so impressed. I don't suppose I could have a copy, could I? I think I'd like to quote your work in my lecture series."

"Of course. It's the least I can do. You've been so kind to me today. I'll email it to you."

"Well, if King's don't bite your hand off, I will."

Uncharacteristically and irrationally, Matthew surprised himself and seized the opportunity to extend their neonate union. Whist their relationship had not extended beyond formal academic discourse, Matthew wondered if he could summon the fortitude to attempt a foray into more personal territory.

"I think you will be great tomorrow. They'll love you. I'm only sorry I won't be there to see your triumph."

"Flattery, Matthew. Keep it up. I need all the encouragement I can get."

"Seriously, it is great. I'm not surprised they invited you. Good work, Susan." He hoped his compliment had sounded to Susan less patronising that it had done to him.

"Thanks."

"So, how about dinner tonight, then? I know some good eateries round here."

"Nice idea, but apparently I'm to attend *Formal Hall* this evening. I'm told it is a special dinner held each week for Fellows. It sounds all a bit like Harry Potter and Hogwarts to me, but I can't wait. Come to think of it, I'm going to dash now. I'm going to see if I can get a power-nap and a shower before dinner."

"Yes, I don't blame you. Tomorrow? Fancy a guided tour of Cambridge."

"Sounds great, but all my expenses allow for is a flight in cattle class to get here, then one night in halls, then deliver the paper and then straight back on the red-eye. But thanks. Tell you what, let's exchange contacts and maybe we can hook up next time you are in Ottawa."

"Sure. A bit of a whistle-stop tour, then?"

"Yeah. Funny how when my boss does an international keynote he seems to stay for a whole week and go sightseeing. I'm afraid I'm just a minion, so I'm on a cheap, quick turnaround."

"Sounds familiar. Anyway, good luck tomorrow – not that you need it. I've got some writing to catch up on anyway. Like you I guess, if you don't keep publishing, you're out on your ear."

"Tell me about it. Anyway, thanks for today. Especially for the punting. It really made my trip. Now I must love you and leave you."

Susan raised herself up, provided a half-sincere cheek kiss, an awkward hug and then left. Left the room, left the college and left Matthew to lick his wounds and to rehearse a fabricated version as to why he had only asked her to dinner out of politeness and not out of desire. Finally, to divert his injured ego, he raised the lid on his laptop and began adding notes to the college servers. Notes that bore an uncanny resemblance to the minutiae of the paper that Susan would be delivering to a lecture hall full of post-graduates at King's College in approximately eighteen hours' time. Plagiarism was condemned as an act of moral turpitude, but sharing ideas was to be encouraged and sharing is what he convinced himself he was engaged in as his mind raced and his fingers attempted to follow as he rattled the laptop keyboard. These notes would dual as a chapter in his book and a seminar which would be slotted into his teaching timetable and delivered in a month.

That no contact details had been exchanged was a thought that Matthew concealed behind the pages of academic prose which flowed from his fingers and into his laptop and from there into the servers where it would be embalmed for future generations of undergraduates to admire.

As he walked his way back from his rooms on the second floor of the esteemed dons' accommodation block to his home, he watched the enthusiasm of self-entitled Cambridge students confidently routing themselves to their favoured drinking establishments to lubricate their erudition.

Entering his front door, collecting a handful of bills from the mat and pouring an overly large glass of wine felt burdensome. Selecting an LP of *Max Richter's Voices*, lowering the stylus onto the black vinyl and then lowering himself into the armchair which retained his imprint felt lonely. Loneliness gripped Matthew. Loneliness became the precursor for despondency and desolation.

As the hypnotic tones of Max Richter's haunting masterpiece began to float around Matthew's living room and the superimposed words of the United Nations Declaration of

Human Rights, which cleverly overlaid the musical notation, he contemplated how little the human race had achieved towards the aims expressed by the carefully constructed prose and his desolation amplified.

> *"We the Peoples of the United Nations, determined to reaffirm faith in fundamental human rights, in the dignity and worth of the human person, in the equal rights of men and women and of nations large and small..." "All human beings are born free and equal in dignity and rights."*

He knew the desolate emotions which had begun shrouding him all too well and he knew how to deflect them. His intellectual pursuits were sufficient to subordinate feelings of personal inadequacy, failure and hopelessness. He gulped his wine, reached for his laptop and the next chapter of his book continued forming from the reflections he carried around like an encyclopaedic archive of experiences, readings and encounters. His existing knowledge would become embroidered by his seminar discussions and his cerebral engagement with Susan as the words formed sentences, the sentences formed paragraphs and the paragraphs filled page after page with intellect for him to revisit and refine. Susan and Heidi disappeared behind a wall of exposition and time rebooted itself in order to redirect him to the comfort of routine. Lectures, writing, seminars and faculty meetings would replace emotion and Matthew would return to safety.

The only fracture in his comfort was the endless preparation needed for the South African field trip scheduled for later in the year which, whilst routine enough, planning for visits to Khayelitsha reminded him of Heidi and not being reminded of Heidi was his intent but ultimately his failure. Susan had filled a few hours with stimulation and fraternisation, but in Heidi he still found unsettling prurience.

Another chapter of his new book found completion on the laptop screen as he absorbed the events of the day.

Defining human and civil rights: The jurisprudence of the United Nations Declaration of Human Rights at domestic and international levels and its influence on global social media

May – Judith

May felt tedious and repetitive and Matthew longed for new companionship to quelle the tide of emotional remoteness that memories of Heidi inflicted on him and which had come to dominate his life. Once more, that bench on that green on the first day of another month fostered a sense of forlornness that was hard to quell. Wanting a companion to share his life with had preoccupied his thoughts and stymied his academic creativity. Heidi had drifted into his mind so many times and then just as quickly dispelled by his well-rehearsed mental techniques designed to convince himself that she was not intruding into his consciousness. Even the acanthus, hardy geraniums and aquilegias, which were taking their turn to brighten the flower beds on that Cambridge green, failed to penetrate the Cimmerian mist which had taken control of his disposition.

His stare became fixed and his mind became anchored as a woman of about his age joined him on the bench. Matthew's attention was first drawn to a miniature bulldog nuzzling his ankle. As his eyes followed the bulldog's lead to its owner, he became aware of a slim, sharply handsome, middle-aged woman glaring across the green apparently oblivious of Matthew and unconcerned about the close proximity to him that her canine charge had achieved. Her hair was short cropped and her fingernails manicured crudely with gregarious colours. Matthew found himself briefly scrutinising and then analysing her clothes, her shoes and her handbag. Routine character analysis formed easily in

Matthew's mind but the need to escape the attention of the dog overrode his desire to assess and catalogue the stranger.

Matthew embraced the cue to leave and began packing his thoughts away ready to head to his rooms at St Michael's and to begin the next chapter of his book which was to address post-nationalism in the twenty first century. His forethought was abruptly disrupted by the anonymous dog owner as she tugged firstly at the lead and then at Matthew's attention.

"Don't mind Bunter, he's harmless. Not mine actually. I'm just walking him for a friend during my lunchbreak." Then, looking up, she continued. "Look at them. Terrible, isn't it?"

"Huh? I'm sorry? What?"

"Them over there. Terrible, isn't it? Hundreds of them."

"Hundreds of what?"

"Poles!"

"Huh? Flag poles?"

"No. Them over there. Poles from Poland. Hundreds of them. Coming here taking our jobs."

"Excuse me?"

"The country is full of them. Everywhere you go. The sooner they go home the better. If it isn't the Poles, it's the muslins."

Matthew knew better than to challenge this assumption but failed to stop himself.

"I think you mean Muslims. Muslin is a material. A Muslim is someone who follows Islam."

"Yeah, that's what I said. Muslins and them Poles too."

Well, actually *they* do a really good job here. *They* are really important to our economy."

"Really? You one of those re-moaners? One of those woke lefties? They don't do no good. Take our jobs. British jobs should be for British people, I say. No good ever came of the EU. It's going to break up now 'cos of Brexit, you know. It can't carry on without us Brits."

"Well, I doubt that, but if it does break up then it won't be because we left. The chances of the UK breaking up are much higher right now."

"Bloody nonsense. I read it in the Express. The EU is as good as finished now. Good riddance, I say."

"I think you'll find it's not finished yet by a long shot."

"No. I read it. It was on the front page of the Daily Express."

Matthew checked himself to stem the rising bile in his gut and to restrain his instinct to fire insults at his unwelcome bench-companion. He knew that any academic analysis of the relationship between the UK and the EU and the negative impact of the cessation of freedom of movement of goods, people and services on the UK economy would be no match for the impact of a single, misleading headline on the front of the Daily Express. His published and lorded paper on the anthropological perspectives of immigrant labour on the socio-economic structures of the UK was no match for newspaper headline writers, but rationality deserted him and he fell headlong into conflict.

"In actual fact, we rely on immigrant labour to support just about every aspect of our society from health care to the NHS, to the food and medical supply chains, not to mention the service industry. Music, arts, research, sciences all rely to a greater or lesser extent on immigrants."

"They come over here, get a job in the NHS and then go on the sick. They are just bleeding us dry. Why should I pay my taxes just for them to sit around at my expense? I pay my taxes; they just live on benefits."

"I'm sorry. That's simply not true."

"Don't be sorry, dear, it is totally true. I should know. My son works in the NHS and he told me."

"Can I ask what your son does? Is he a doctor?"

"No, he's a cleaner. He says nearly everyone is foreign. He says the nurses can hardly speak English. It's just not right."

"I'm sure they can speak English or they wouldn't get a job."

"No, my son says they can't speak English. They train in their own country then come over here and take jobs from our nurses."

"Why would they do that?"

"Better pay."

"Actually, the truth is that it is very expensive to train doctors and nurses so we let other countries pay for the training and then we just recruit them. We simply buy them in cheap. That's where the problem lies. They are not coming over here taking jobs. We buy them cheap to fill the jobs that we don't have doctors and nurses of our own for."

"That's just immoral. Now we are out of the EU we can train our own doctors and nurses."

Matthew felt himself losing the argument.

"Well, we could always train our own nurses. We just don't train enough, so we buy them in cheap in order to save money. We don't have enough nurses at all now we've left the EU. But my point is, you are blaming the EU for the UK government's policy on nursing recruitment."

"Anyway, all that mass immigration has stopped now."

"What mass immigration?"

"All those Europeans flooding in taking our jobs."

"But, but, but, freedom of movement and immigration are different things. Not to mention refugees which is different again."

"That's my point. They just keep coming. Now we can control our borders and stop mass immigration."

"Where do you get all this from?"

"The government said so. That's why I voted Leave."

"Actually, the government was backing Remain. You are just quoting the Vote Leave campaign slogans."

"Well, anyway, now we can control our own borders and our own money."

"Look, we weren't in the Schengen area so we could always control our own borders and we weren't in the Eurozone so we always controlled our own currency."

"Who are you? One of those socialite teachers, or something?"

"I think you mean socialist. I'm Matthew. I'm a lecturer here in Cambridge. And I don't think a label like *socialist* is very helpful. I'm just talking facts not ideology."

"Talking bollocks, more like. I'm Judith by the way."

"I'm Matthew. Well, anyway, Judith, I think I must be going. Goodbye."

"Me too. I've got to get back to work."

"OK. I'd like to say that is has been nice talking to you, Judith, but I'd be lying."

"Huh? Well, it's been nice teaching you some home truths. Bye, Matthew."

Matthew grasped the moral high ground but conceded defeat and raised himself to head back to St Michael's College. Judith raised herself and matched his stride in the same direction. Matthew was unable to hide the disappointment in his voice and found words to match his emotional ire.

"Oh. Shit. I see we are going in the same direction."

"Looks like it. Where are you going?"

"St Michael's College. You?"

"St Michael's College. Small world. I work in the canteen on the till."

"Small world indeed, Judith. I lecture there."

"Yes, I know. You don't recognise me, do you, Matthew?"

"Should I?"

"Well, I've worked in the canteen for five years and served you with a flat white and a croissant just about every day."

"Oh, dear God. Yes. Of course I know you. I am so very sorry."

"Don't worry. I'm used to being invisible. You lot are always too busy talking about something really important to be bothered with the likes of me."

"I promise you, Judith. We talk a load of crap all the time. You are much more important."

"Yes. I know I am. I listen to you lot and you talk total bullshit. But I'm still invisible so don't pretend that you care about me."

"I promise to do better. I'll make a point of saying hello to you."

"Why? Because you have to?"

"I didn't mean it like that."

"Maybe not, but that's how it is. Just think, if Remain hadn't just ignored me then I might have voted for them. As it was, Vote Leave spoke my language. It was like they spoke to me personally. It felt like I wasn't invisible. That Farage bloke too. He was the same. He told me what I wanted to hear."

"Christ. You've hit the nail on the head there. Can I quote you?"

"You can do what you like, darling. The fact is, I'm working out my notice. I leave in a month, thank God. I'm done with all you lefty lot talking bollocks and treating me like crap. I've got a job as a Teaching Assistant in a primary school. At least the kids won't ignore me there. They'll call me, Miss. They'll show me a bit of respect. Anyway, it looks like we are walking back to college together, so I can carry on persuading you why we are so much better now we are out of the EU."

"You can try, but look, Judith, let me ask you a simple question."

"OK."

"Just give me one example how your life is better being out of the EU."

"Easy. We can control our borders, control our currency and make our own laws."

"No, we already did all that. We were always sovereign. The EU is actually made up of sovereign states. But I didn't mean that. I meant how is *your* life better? *You* personally."

"Well, it doesn't really make any difference to me personally, darling."

"So why did you vote to leave?"

"To stop all the immigrants taking our jobs."

"But Judith, we've been here already. You voted Leave because Vote Leave told you there was mass immigration and that wages would go up if we left and because the NHS would get more money. But now we are out none of that is true. They called the Remain campaign 'project fear', but now all the 'project fear' stuff is coming true. We don't have enough workers in the NHS, enough fruit pickers, enough lorry drivers, the NHS isn't getting any more money, wages aren't going up, inflation is taking off and GDP has taken a massive hit."

"I know. I'm not stupid."

"Huh? Well, why did you vote to leave the EU, then?"

"I told you. British jobs for British people."

"You are just repeating the slogans again. Look, let me ask you another question. As a country we are less well off. That means you are less well off. That is a fact and that is the government saying that. You've also lost your freedom of movement. So, are you glad that we have left or do you regret it?"

"To be honest, I regret it. I think we were much better off in the EU except for the mass immigration."

"Oh, Judith. The EU was not responsible for mass immigration. We weren't even in the Schengen Area. Look, we are going round in circles. So, if you regret leaving, would you vote to Remain now if we had another referendum?"

"Oh, no, I'd still vote to leave."

"But Judith, you just said you regret having voted to leave. So why vote to leave, then?"

"Well, we had a referendum so we have to stick to it. That's democracy."

"Yes, I get your point, but what I meant was that if there was a brand-new referendum and you knew what you know now and you had the chance to stay in the EU, would you change your vote to Remain?"

"No, I just told you. British jobs for British people."

"Oh, Judith. Do you even know what that really means?"

"Of course. It's obvious. Looks like you having all those letters after your name doesn't make you very smart."

"Actually, Judith, you might have a point there. I'll concede that."

"Anyway, it's me that is talking facts and you that's talking bollocks."

"Oh, Judith, that's not true."

"Why? 'Cos you've got letters after your name and I serve coffee. Is that why you are right and I'm wrong?"

"I didn't say that."

"It's what you meant. You reckon all Leavers are thick, don't you? Look, Matthew, as far as Brexit is concerned, I believed what Vote Leave said. That's why I voted for them."

"But they were lying."

"Were they? Or maybe they meant it even if they can't deliver it now."

"So, it's a matter of trust rather than honesty, then. You just voted for who you trusted rather than what they said."

"Maybe. There's nothing wrong in that. Anyway, if you remember, more than half the country believed in what they said and I reckon whatever it is that most people believe in makes it right. Makes it facts."

"So, what you are saying is that a fact is no more than a communal belief."

"If you say so."

"You know, Judith, you might just be quoting, or at least misquoting Karl Popper."

"You are off on one again, aren't you?"

"Yeah. Popper rejected the classical inductivist views on scientific method in favour of empirical falsification. According to him, a theory in the empirical sciences can never be proven, but it can be falsified. Popper was opposed to the classical justifications account of knowledge, which he replaced with critical rationalism."

"That's all just mumbo jumbo. I just know what I believe and most people agreed with me over Brexit. So, it makes you and your beliefs a minority. So that makes me right and you wrong. Plus, it's democracy, isn't it? When we left the EU, we got what most people believed in."

"Well, yes, but what if what they believed in has now been proved to be wrong. Truth and falsehoods aren't a matter of democracy."

"Well, actually, they are. Free society, free speech and democracy. We got what we wanted. Just because it isn't what you want doesn't make it wrong. Just because they can't deliver what they said doesn't make them liars."

"But ..."

"But nothing, Matthew. If you don't mind me saying, if you just learnt to speak plain English, then maybe you'd understand it when you heard it."

"Point taken, Judith. Christ, I reckon you'd run rings around my students."

Silence followed Matthew and Judith until their return to St Michael's College. Judith content that she had won the argument; Matthew conflicted between the paradigms of fact and falsehood in political discourse.

"So, Judith, here we are. Back at college. I'll see you around, then."

"OK. Any time you want sorting out you know where to find me."

"Seriously, though. That was a very refreshing chat. Thanks."

"Any time."

Matthew and his streetwise adversary parted company and headed to their different worlds within the same building. Matthew left with his thoughts and Judith left with Bunter. He knew he would deliberately avoid conversation with Judith. He knew her views were entrenched, irrational and irreversible and he disliked the discomfort she inflicted on what he considered to be his intelligent analysis of immigrants and their worth to society and to the economy. Above all, he was unsettled by her intransigent credibility. She represented the new order in what was often charactered as *Brexit Britain* and he was disquieted by it. *"Great Britain is in conflict with Little England,"* he quipped silently to himself.

Reaching his rooms, Matthew again sought companionship from his laptop and began exploring the power of political propaganda. Judith had just written a chapter of his book in which she would be relentlessly quoted and analysed.

Sloganising in political campaigning: a discourse and critical analysis of campaign slogans in the EU referendum

June – Kayla

The inevitability of Matthew greeting the first day of June on that bench on that green once again brought indistinct but familiar feelings of dysphoria. Another writing day began with emptiness and lack lustre thoughts of the next chapter of his book which was to explore societal change and the *eco-culture* of the twenty first century. The morning had been spent staring at an unwelcoming laptop screen whilst his thoughts swirled around never resting on the subject matter. Having failed at stirring any interesting, let alone inspiring words, he had located himself on that bench on that green to accept the solace that the peonies, roses and sweet peas offered his senses. The flora decorating Jesus Green added effortlessly to the chromaticity of the environment but failed in their attempt to brighten his aura.

The more Matthew strained his intellect, the less his academic mind offered any words worthy of inspection. The first day of each month was dedicated to writing and his career depended upon him creating new and challenging enlightenment. He knew his career progression was determined solely by each article he produced. *"I'm only ever as good as my last gig. The last thing I write will be the only thing I'll be judged on,"* he thought soberly.

As his mind drifted away from its intended course, thoughts of Heidi again began their monthly intrusion until his serenity was brutally interrupted by the two words he dreaded most when he was seeking the calm that he knew he needed for words and sentences to construct themselves in his mind.

"Hello, Sir."

Looking up he focussed firstly on a pair of iridescent orange running shoes before his eyes drifted upwards inspecting a pair of slender legs barely hidden by loud, skin-tight, paella-coloured leggings. Further inspection included a stretch top hugging the contours of a young, female body and emphasising surprisingly erect nipples. An iPhone was strapped to an arm, EarPods were suspended in each ear and some sort of computerised watch blinked as it monitored the bodily functions of the nymphette disturbing his contemplation.

"Oh, hi. Sorry, I was miles away. Kayla, isn't it?"

"Yes, that's right, Sir. Not disturbing you, am I, Sir?"

"Yes, you bloody well are," he thought whilst forcing a smile onto his lips. "No, not at all. How are you?" he heard himself speak with discompassionate detachment.

"Great, thanks." Then, after sitting abruptly down angled towards Matthew, she threw one leg up onto the bench between them to display her neat pudenda, barely hidden by stretched lycra, before continuing. "OK if I join you for a minute, Sir?"

"Oh, dear God. No. Just jog on and leave me in peace. Start jogging and keep jogging until I never see you again," his mind screamed to itself. Matthew failed to find the words his subconscious demanded before summoning a transparent misrepresentation of his thoughts. "No problem. There's plenty of room."

"Any chance I can pick your brains for a minute, Sir? My dissertation is due in in a month and I've hit a bit of a block."

Matthew submitted to the inevitability of a nineteen-year-old student wanting to ingratiate herself with her lecturer who would be grading her work and which would ultimately determine her success at university and therefore open or close doors for the rest of her life. Matthew understood this dance well and accepted his responsibility. He knew he was the gatekeeper to the successful or unsuccessful completion of his degree course and that the outcome would determine career paths for his young students. He acknowledged his responsibility and knew he would play his part as requested. However, contrary thoughts filled his head. *"No, leave me alone. That's what we have seminars for. Just go away. I have writing to do and I'm struggling too. Just leave me alone."* Then, the words formed and the words he spoke became accompanied by a forced smile. "Of course. What can I do for you?"

"Well, Sir …. actually, do you mind if I drop the, 'Sir', thingy? It really smacks of some sort of outmoded patriarchy. Can I call you Matt?"

"No. Call me, Sir. That's the unwritten rule. I call you by your first name when we are in a tutorial, by your surname when we are in a lecture and you call me Sir. That way I can patronise you and demonstrate my superiority over you." Matthew's thoughts again secreted themselves and his response was ambivalent enough for Kayla to force her ingress into his protective space.

"Well, Matthew, not Matt."

"OK. So, Matthew, in your last lecture you talked a lot about what you called the *demiurge society*. It really got me thinking."

"Glad to hear it, Kayla. It's kind of what you are here for. *Thinking* has always been a prerequisite for Cambridge students."

"Yeah. It was really stimulating. I just love your lectures."

"Creep," thought Matthew.

Ignoring or choosing ambivalence to Matthew's sarcasm, Kayla continued. "Anyway. Have I got this right? You are re-tasking the word demiurge from its original meaning of a supernatural being who creates a universe to a modern context where, rather than we create a universe, we have to reinvent it before it is too late?"

"That's actually very impressive, Kayla, but I'm not sure about the word reinvent."

"No, sorry. That doesn't do it justice. I guess one word alone is insufficient. What I meant was that since *you* have fucked up the planet, then it is now down to *me* to save it. So, I am the demiurge in this scenario. Sorry about saying fuck."

"Let's ignore the reference to the 'f' word, shall we? Well, I don't think I can take full credit alone for screwing up the planet and maybe it will take more than just you to sort it out, but yes."

"No, by 'you' I meant you and your generation and by 'me' I meant me and my generation."

"Yes, I was being facetious. I got that. But even so, you can't blame my generation alone. You can easily go back to the industrial revolution and the rise of capitalism."

"Yeah, or you can go back even further to the pre-industrial society that cultured the need for individual and collective wealth creation."

"Indeed. That's pretty insightful. I'm genuinely impressed. Well done, Kayla. I guess you were listening to my lecture." Matthew's words had begun to adopt a tone of genuine engagement as he chose to accept ownership of his student's intellectual insights.

"Right, so if I represent the demiurge generation, then the big question is, how am I going to reverse all the damage of previous generations? Because, frankly, if I don't, then there won't be any future generations. So, this demiurge culture thingy is kind of the big question of my generation."

"Well put, Kayla, but if I may suggest, try to find a better expression than *culture thingy* when you are writing your dissertation."

"Right. What about a *demiurge culture shift*?"

"Not bad. Work on that."

Matthew quickly realigned her words into, a *systemic demiurgic paradigm shift,* as the germ of the chapter that had so far concealed itself from him began to become fertilised. Of course, he knew that he should share this thought with his student, but the imperative to publish new and erudite words trumped the need for him to educate the post-pubescent, lycra-clad starlet forcing the curvature of her toned body into his space.

"Right. Great. So far so good, Matthew. Which brings me to my proposition. I, Kayla, alone, can't change the world, but collectively we can. So how does the shift from 'I' to 'we' come about?"

"That is the exact question. Well done, Kayla."

Again, Matthew filed Kayla's words for refining and publishing.

"Because, ultimately, it has to be down to politicians across the world to sit down and to agree a solution."

"Ah, forgive me, Kayla, but after a promising start, you have now fallen into the simplicity trap and simplicity is simply telling you to pass the buck. It can't always be someone else's problem to sort out."

"Wow. Yeah. Exactly. If we share the planet then we share the problem and we must therefore share the responsibility for finding and implementing a solution."

"Nicely put."

More words began aligning into sentences and paragraphs in the next chapter of this book.

"So, I guess the biggest question of all is, how do we reach the shift to *all*. How do we move from competition to collaboration?"

"Or is it from capitalism and free market ideology to socialism and command economy?"

"Christ. You are sounding a bit Marxist there, if I may say so, Matthew. You almost went from capitalism to communism."

"No, not so. But might we consider a paradigm shift from capitalism to communalism?"

"I see what you did there. Communalism not communism. You removed the political overtone there, didn't you?"

"I'm just propositioning in order to provoke you, Kayla. After all, you are the demiurge, not me. And ultimately it is down to you, not me, to write your dissertation."

"OK, Matthew, so collective or communal responsibility, then? We must all embrace the demiurge culture change."

"Good work, Kayla, but you need to go deeper."

Kayla leaned inwards to Matthew to express interest and to project her breasts and spread her legs wider to offer him an invitation deeper into her sexually charged academic discourse.

"This is seriously interesting. I'm so glad I bumped into you. I really want to tease out some ideas about this global culture shift thingy."

"Again, Kayla. Avoid the word *thingy*."

"Sorry. No more thingies. Anyway, have you got another few minutes?"

"Not really," thought Matthew. "Yes, of course," he said.

"Great. Follow me. Come on. Let's sort the world out by the river. I've got some vegan falafel in my backpack. We can share. It's the least I can do to thank you for this private audience."

Whilst Matthew contemplated the fact that falafels were always vegan and therefore didn't require the prefix *vegan,*

Kayla stood up, turned and strutted with overly long strides towards the river bank without waiting for Matthew's acceptance. Matthew was snagged more by her flirtation than her academic prowess as his eyes obediently followed the shiny, body-perfect sprite. However, he acknowledged to himself that the combination of both her sexual heat and her academic stimulation was exhilarating.

Foregoing the professional reticence that he knew was required, Matthew found himself reclining on the banks of the River Cam facing an undeniably attractive and flirtatious nineteen-year-old student whose attire made little attempt to hide the overtly sexual display of her body that she had knowingly and deliberately presented to him. He knew that the panorama in which he and Kayla were actors would inevitably raise eyebrows in the Dean's office should a grudge-laden student decide to capture the event on a smart phone for future sharing on the college intranet as revenge for a poor grade on an assignment. However, his attraction to Kayla was undeniable and her barely disguised libidinous provocation was heady and intoxicating. Even so, he scanned the vicinity to ensure that prying eyes were not interpreting the amorous interaction for the fact that it was exactly that despite being cloaked in academic discourse.

Matthew's tone became soft and seductive. "Where were we, Kayla?"

"We were just going to share falafels before solving all global problems."

"Indeed. It's not easy saving the planet on an empty stomach. Are you sure you have enough?"

"Yeah, of course. Here. Try this."

Without qualm, Kayla produced a falafel from her backpack and pushed it to Matthew's mouth. Matthew's lips parted willingly and accepted the offering whilst engaging her eyes and meeting her well-rehearsed flirtatious grin. He knew the dance was being choreographed by his student and knew he had to stop it – but not yet.

"Anyway, Matt. Back to the demiurge thingy."

Matthew noted and accepted the transition from Matthew to Matt and welcomed the step change towards further intimacy.

"Again Kayla. Drop the 'thingy' bit."

"Yeah. Sorry, Matt. So, anyway, back to the - the – er – *demiurge paradigm.*"

"Yes, the *demiurge paradigm.*" The title to the next chapter of his book just wrote itself.

"Well, we have to shift the paradigm from 'I' to 'we' to effect any meaningful change."

"Yes, that's right. But how?"

"Well, it's the politicians who effect the change, so, I guess it is up to us to elect politicians who will take climate change seriously. That would be 'us' using democracy to effect meaningful change."

"So far, so good. Continue."

Kayla helped herself to another falafel and simultaneously offered another to Matthew.

Turning away from Matthew and raising her eyes to denote a sudden epiphany, Kayla continued her stream of erudite consciousness. "Oh, I get it. That's both the solution and the problem, isn't it?"

"Keep that thought going, Kayla," Matthew demanded with a hint of urgency, hoping he might discover the crux of the next chapter of his book.

"Well, I guess there are two things that spring to mind. Firstly, even if we elect a government on a climate ticket, we have to trust them to deliver what they promise and that is a big ask. Most politicians say whatever they have to, to get elected, then do the opposite."

"OK, and secondly?"

"Well, we live in a democracy – sort of. But not all countries are so lucky. In some countries there is a dictatorship and there is no collective 'we' to make any change. Since climate change is a global issue then all countries have to work in accord. Or, more specifically, all world leaders have to work in accord in a culture of trust. And that is one giant ask."

"Exactly so. Well done, Kayla. Then why don't they?"

"That's an easy one, Matt. Because countries compete with one another. In fact, nationalism is kind of on the rise at the moment. They compete for resources and power. And to do that they will always do whatever is necessary to gain dominance. And climate change policy just slides down their agendas. So basically, we are all fucked. Sorry, I just said fuck again, didn't I?"

"Don't worry about the 'f' word. Just don't use it in your dissertation. It's frowned upon. But otherwise, what you are saying is excellent, Kayla. Keep that going and you have the start of a good dissertation."

"Thanks. So, all I need to do is to work out how to make all global leaders work in harmony with each other without competing. I need to convince them all to drop the twin ideologies of free market economics and libertarianism."

"Indeed. Do that and I'll give you an 'A' for your dissertation. In fact, I'll also nominate you for a Nobel Peace Prize."

"OK. I'll be the demiurge who shifts the paradigm from 'I' to 'we' globally. Thanks, Matt. That's great. Here, have another falafel."

Kayla pushed a final falafel into Matthew's receptive mouth and followed the intrusion by licking her fingers in a display of exaggerated seduction. Then, as he leaned in to embrace the courtship dance that he knew he should reject, Kayla jumped up, swung her backpack over her shoulders and, without looking back, chirped a farewell and jogged along the riverbank and out of view leaving Matthew to nurse his bruised ego content in the knowledge that he now had the next chapter of his book in his mind ready to commit to the college servers. He even amused himself imagining that Kayla would be quoting passages from *The Demiurge Paradigm Shift* chapter when she submitted her final dissertation for him to assess. A student as perceptive as Kaya would be intelligent enough to quote her lecturer in her dissertation in order to maximise her chances of a high grade.

Satisfied that his writing day would again produce enough words to satiate the adamic appetite of the university, Matthew marshalled his thoughts into order and set off back to his rooms in St Michael's College to find the solitude he needed to summon erudition into coherent sentences worthy of the status expected of him. Words, sentences, paragraphs and finally a chapter filled the screen of his laptop and committed itself to the college server alongside his other acclaimed missives.

The demiurge paradigm shift: contradictions in globalism and the imperative to construct a plurality policy

July – Eva

The recent rain had brought the phlox and shockingly orange marigolds into bloom lightening Matthew's spirit with a riot of colour as he strolled across that green to find his place on that bench on the first day of July. His progress was halted by the sight of Eva already occupying his seat. Except, this was a different Eva. This was an Eva with rounded shoulders and tear-stained cheeks. This was a deeply distressed Eva. This was an Eva to avoid at all cost in order to avoid her disquiet.

His first instinct was to flee rather than allow himself to be drawn into her remorse. However, Eva's eyes flicked up from their bland stare and caught Matthew's with a desperate glance before returning to their remoteness. Matthew knew this was an invitation and he knew that he wished to decline the offer to join her but he was snagged like a foul-hooked salmon and stepped slowly towards his troubled friend.

"Eva? Are you OK?"

His trite but essential salutation allowed his distressed admirer to lie in order to reel him in with consummate and rehearsed ease. With practised sadness in her voice, she tugged on the line and Matthew was irretrievably landed.

"Yes, I'm fine."

"Really?"

"No. I'm shit actually."

As his limited powers of verbosity rose to the challenge and then deserted him, he sank from triteness to banality.

"Can I help?"

"No, there's nothing you can do. There's nothing anyone can do."

"OK. I'm not going to intrude. I'm just going to sit here in silence. I can see you are upset. If you want to talk, then I'm here. If not, I'll understand. If you just want to sit in silence, then I'll sit in silence with you."

Matthew quietened himself and offered himself a compliment for what he considered was gentle empathy, but Eva, having been extended the invitation, chose not to wait further before snaring Matthew.

"Oh, Matthew. It's just so awful. It's Dave."

"Dave? Your boyfriend?"

"More than a boyfriend, Matthew. I moved in with him earlier this year. Soon after that New Year's Eve party, actually. After he got back from America, he invited me to move in with him. He said he couldn't bare being parted from me. I really thought he was my *foreva fella*."

"Oh. Has he ... you know ... has he left you?"

Matthew cringed at his blunt ineptitude as his prior attempt at gentle empathy escaped him. Once again, the verbose eloquence he possessed when cornered in an academic debate deserted him leaving him with little more than desperate and inappropriate vapidity. Furthermore, he stiffened at the thought that Eva might now try to entrap him on a rebound.

"No, Matthew. He's dead."

"Jesus! Fuck! I'm so sorry. Forgive me. What? No!"

"Forgive you? What for? For being the usual twat that you are? Don't worry, I'm used to that."

"Eva. I don't know what to say." Matthew now spoke the only truth he had found.

"It only took a month."

"What?"

"He was diagnosed with testicular cancer. Then he was dead in a month. Funny how one life can be taken and another shattered in a month."

"Eva, I'm just so sorry. Is there anything I can do? Anything at all?"

"Just sit here for a minute. I came to sit on this bench to get away. To get away from all the sympathy and awkwardness that everyone seems to think I need. I wanted to find some privacy. Everyone has been so nice but I just felt suffocated. I just had to be on my own. Then, as soon as I was on my own, I was crushed by loneliness. Can you just sit with me for a bit?"

"Of course. For as long as you like." Matthew sank into that bench on that green and dismissed further thoughts of writing another chapter of his book despite this being the allocated day for him to find scholarly words to impress his peers and to satisfy the stifling targets set for him by the college hierarchy.

"Do you want to know what else is funny, Matthew?"

"What?"

"Because we weren't actually married, people don't really care about me much."

"I'm sure that's not true."

"I'm afraid it is, Matthew. To 'lose a husband' is a *thing*. It is a definite *thing*. It is a thing everyone understands and sympathises with. To 'lose a boyfriend' – not so much of a *thing* apparently."

"No, I'm sure everyone cares just as much."

"You'd think, wouldn't you, but it has been a harsh lesson for me. Losing him was bad enough, but finding out I don't matter was a real shock. It's like I don't exist anymore. His family and friends just took over. I was pushed out."

"I don't understand, Eva."

"Well, I guess you've never been in this situation. The fact is, he really was just a boyfriend. What's more, I had only just moved in with him. So, his family got to decide everything about his funeral, they got the inheritance, they got to grieve. I got to be a spectator. I got nothing. I didn't seem to count."

"I'm sure that's not …."

"Don't say it again, Matthew. Come on, you are the famous anthropologist. You explain it. If he'd been my husband I would have been at the centre of people's concern. I would have inherited the house. I would have been his legacy. As a girlfriend I was nothing. We were as much of a couple as if we were married, but I got left behind with nothing as soon as he died. I wasn't even allowed to be alone with him in his final hours. They all just took over as though I didn't really count. They were his mother and his father and his sister. They had labels which meant they were front and centre. I was just 'the girlfriend'. Being the girlfriend is just not the same. I immediately became invisible. Even the hospital wouldn't share details with me because I wasn't *family*. Do you know what hurts the most, Matthew? I can't even call myself a widow, because technically I'm not."

"Christ, Eva. I'd never even thought about it."

"No. No-one ever does. I'm just the ignored girlfriend. Explain it to me Matthew. Why does the word *wife* carry such wait and why does being a wife allow you to adopt the word *widow*? Why does the word *girlfriend* mean almost nothing? Dave and I were the same people in the same relationship but because we decided not to get married, I'm now a non-person."

"I'm sure that's not ..."

"True? Are you really going to say that again despite me sitting here as living proof that it is true?"

"No. I'm not going to say it again. I believe you. I'm just at a loss for words."

"Don't worry, you are not alone. No-one knows what to say to me. So, they stopped bothering. The tragedy is, that we were planning on getting married later this year but hadn't told anyone."

"I'm so sorry."

"Stop saying that. Do you want to know the worst?"

"Go on."

"Not only were we going to get married; I'm pregnant."

"Christ! Eva!"

"Yup. I'm eight weeks pregnant. I found out the same time he got his diagnosis."

"But surely his family would want to treat you like their own then."

"If they knew, maybe. But they just pushed me aside. I haven't told them. I don't want to tell them. This is my baby. Mine and David's. Not theirs. They got everything else, so this is *my* baby. They can all go to hell."

Silence drew them inexorably into the space that separated them on that bench until Matthew accepted his role in her life as a longstanding friend and confidante.

"Right, Eva. I don't know how, but I didn't know that any of this was going on. I think I bury myself in my work and shut out people who really matter. Again, and I really mean it, I'm sorry. I've been a very bad friend. For that I am deeply sorry."

"Don't worry. I think I just became invisible."

"Look. I'm cancelling everything. You've got me for the day. In fact, you've got me for as long as you want. I'm going to be a good friend now. How about we walk and talk? Just that. Walk and talk."

"Thanks Matthew. I think I really need a friend right now."

"You don't have to say it. I've not been a good friend. We've known each other, well, forever, and yet all this was going on in your life and I didn't even know. I am so, so sorry."

"Let's agree on something, Matthew. You stop saying you are sorry and I won't punch you in the face. Let's take it as read that you are sorry, shall we? I get that you feel guilty, but let's face it, you are a total dick and I'm an idiot for having chased after you all these years."

"Fair comment, Eva."

"And, well, as for me sticking my tongue down your throat at the New Year's Eve party, let's pretend that didn't happen, shall we?"

"Agreed."

"Believe it or not, I was very happy with Dave and I'd got over you. I was just a bit drunk. A lot drunk actually. And then, there you were, all alone at midnight. So, let's just call it a pity-snog, shall we?"

The realisation that, in reality, it actually had only been a pity-snog stabbed at the wafer-thin shield that protected his male ego.

"I know. Look, let's not talk about me or even about us. Let's talk about you. Come on. Let's stroll along the river. There are some benches further up. We can find a quiet spot and just talk."

"OK. Just don't expect much sense out of me."

"I expect nothing. But you've got to expect me to be a good friend from now on. OK? As you know, I'll never have the right thing to say, but I'm a good listener."

"Guilty conscience speaking there, Matthew. Don't beat yourself up. You've not been a good friend, but you have been a loyal friend. You've always been there. I guess that's why I had a thing for you. You were like a loyal puppy – a bit annoying, but always there."

"Yes, it is a guilty conscience speaking, but I mean it, I'm going to be your best friend for as long as you can put up with me. Come on, let's go."

Matthew and Eva collected themselves and what was left of their fractured but healing acquaintance together and followed the path of the River Cam as it meandered alongside their conversation.

"You really landed that comment, Eva. The one where you said that you weren't even allowed to be his widow. Wow!"

"I know. It hit me too when I realised it. I'm just the screwed-up girlfriend. That's all."

"Have you had any counselling?"

"Yeah. Work has been really good. They've given me compassionate leave and set up a counsellor for me."

"Any good?"

"Yeah. It's been interesting. But hasn't really helped. Not yet, anyway. Maybe it has. A bit. So, Matthew, don't go all gooey-eyed when I say this, but talking to you is doing much more to help than any counsellor. I'm totally comfortable calling you a twat. I could never say that to my counsellor despite wanting to scream it at her."

"I'm more than happy to be here for you, Eva. What do you mean it was interesting?"

"Well, I banged on about not being able to identify as a widow. I told her that I really needed to be a widow in order to process things and to grieve, but society's view ignored what I wanted. We talked a lot about why I felt that way. She went on about different cultures and how they deal with bereavement. She told me there was only one way to deal with it, and that was whatever way worked for me."

"Good advice."

"She made me realise that it wasn't me who needed to be a widow. It was me who needed others to see me as a widow."

"Sounds like you got a smart counsellor."

"Yeah. She's good. We talked about all sorts of attitudes to death and bereavement. Did you know that in some countries they mourn the death and in other's they celebrate it? Sometimes there are full scale rituals to usher spirits into other worlds."

"Sounds fascinating."

"Yeah. Weirdly, I came out of it identifying as a Buddhist, although I'm not one. Did you know that Buddhists see death as a natural part of the human existence together with the suffering and pain that comes with it? They believe in the here and now and they believe in reincarnation."

"So, you believe in reincarnation?"

"Nope. But it helped a bit to almost believe in it for a while. But no, I don't. Then there was the Jewish *Shiva* where I just remembered all the happy times with him. That helped too. We went through Islamic beliefs, Hindu beliefs, Japanese, Chinese and just about everything."

"And that helped?"

"It was incredible. I ended up analysing my own beliefs about death by touching on loads of different cultural beliefs. I learned a lot about myself."

"And where did you end up?"

"I remember all the good stuff about him. There is no after life other than in my soul. And he'll be there for ever."

"Eva. That's beautiful."

"I also learned that I have to find strength to reinvent myself now. Before he died, I was *Eva and Dave*, Now I'm just Eva. That's the journey I'm on now."

"Tell me about your journey. Tell me about your roadmap."

"They're selling his house. His family are selling the house. They are kicking me out. I'm going to rent an apartment near to the offices where I work. I'll work hard. Rebuild. Eventually find a new person to share my life with. Someone who will accept me and my baby. In short, I'm going to give my life a total spring-clean."

"And I'll be there for you Eva. I'll be there to hold your hand."

"Oh, Matthew, I nearly threw up then. Even for you that was just platitudinous crap. You really have a gift for saying a load of bullshit, don't you? It's one of the things I love about you. No, Matthew. You won't be there for me. Let's just both be honest about that, shall we? Nothing has changed there. Just because you are having a guilt trip doesn't mean you'll suddenly become my bestie."

"I meant it, Eva."

"Yeah, I know you did. Sorry, I don't mean to have a go. But I also know that by this evening you will have moved on again and left me behind. Don't worry, it is not just you. All my so-called friends crowded round me when it happened, but they are all back in their own little worlds now. Just like you will be. I'm not having a go at you; it's just how it is."

"OK, Eva. I'll not try to deny it. But I really do mean it when I say that if ever you want to talk then I will genuinely be there for you. Maybe I can be the one friend that hangs around even if I am a bad friend."

"Thanks. I'll take that. Maybe that makes you my best friend after all."

*****

Matthew and Eva walked, talked and then parted company. Eva headed towards a new, ill-defined life and Matthew headed to his laptop and began typing a new, well-defined chapter.

Cross-cultural aspects of death and bereavement: A conceptual framework within differing societal contexts for comparative analysis

August – Charlotte

Charlotte, from the University of Cape Town had arrived two days ago and had not yet made any attempt to contact Matthew. Her visit was scheduled so that she could lead a short seminar series with Matthew's students in preparation for the forthcoming field trip to Khayelitsha in September. In a month Matthew would be with her in her home town where his amorous affair had taken place. Now, she was in his home town and he desperately wanted a rerun of their carnal encounter. However, the fact that she had not tried to contact him since arriving in Cambridge stabbed at his fragile sense of worth. Furthermore, she had turned down his offer of accommodation and instead had opted for a room in the college guest quarters.

Thoughts of rekindling what had been a passionate encounter dwindled and Matthew was instead left with feelings of abandonment and hopelessness. Even the imposing sunflowers and lilies failed to lift his despondency as he again sat on that bench on that green on the first day of another month.

Matthew glanced at his watch. It was nearly midday. It was approaching what he now billed to be an excruciating reunion with Charlotte. Both he and she were giving up valuable vacation time in order to prepare his students for the fieldtrip which would take place immediately prior to the start of the next term. His mouth began drying, his stomach began churning and aphasia began gripping him as he saw a silhouette of Charlotte approach with a casual gait. As she neared, he raised himself to his feet and forced a smile.

"Hiya, Charlotte."

"Hi, Matthew. Great to see you."

He lunged an awkward hug and a mistimed cheek-kiss at his South African colleague and one-time lover in order to throw camouflage over the inadequacy of his greeting.

"Woah, Matthew! Lovely to see you too. It's nice to be wanted."

"Sorry. I've never been very good at all that hugging and kissing stuff."

"Yes, I know. I remember."

"I've not improved, I'm afraid. And, if I'm honest, I think I am a bit nervous seeing you again."

"Don't be stupid, Matthew. It's cool."

"Ok. Sorry."

As Matthew began filing his chagrin in an overfilled corner of his mind, he allowed himself to scrutinise the being now sitting adjacent to him. Her hair was as black and curly as he remembered. Her body was almost as slender and her eyes still kindled his desire. Her quirky smile still captivated him, but there was something about her demeanour that no longer invited him.

"Anyway, Matthew, look, there's lots to do and not much time, so let's set some ground rules."

"Agreed. So, what happened in Cape Town stays in Cape Town. No need for this to be awkward."

"Er, well it is now, Matthew. I meant ground rules for the seminars."

"Shit. I've done it again, haven't I? Shown myself up as a dork."

"Dork wasn't the word that sprang to mind, Matthew. I was going for *moegoe*."

"Moegoe?"

"Yeah. An Africanism for making a fool of yourself. Shit, sorry, that was cruel."

Matthew considered Charlotte's assessment of his emotional incontinence to be simultaneously overly brutal and completely fair.

"Sorry. I guess my mind was stupidly thinking about what happened when we last met. You are totally right, I'm a complete moegoe."

"OK, I guess we should clear the air. You should know something. I'm with a guy now. He's actually a ranger on Table Mountain. I met him when I climbed the Hiddingh-Ascension with a group of undergrads. It was really tough. His name is Lubanzi. Not my usual type, but we just hit it off. We've been going out for nearly two years now."

"That's great. I'm happy for you." Matthew's mind quickly calculated that 'for nearly two years' meant 'since as soon as he had left'. His stomach joined his mind in squirming.

"Happy for me? Oh, Matthew, you didn't think we …."

"No, don't be silly."

"Oh, you did. Matthew, I'm so sorry. I've been totally insensitive. I just thought we had had a momentary thing. I've not thought about it since."

"Nor me."

"Really? Matthew, I'm not stupid. I'm sorry if you thought that we might pick up where we left off."

"OK. Yes. You are not stupid but clearly I am. Would you be kind enough to move on quickly in order to spare my complete mortification?"

"Yes, please. Let's do that. Look, is there somewhere we can go for lunch? My treat. We can discuss the ground rules for the seminars and eat at the same time."

"Good idea. The Café Cam is just round the corner. Let's grab a table there and forget that I just made a total tit of myself."

"Let's do that. And no, you didn't make a tit of yourself. I'm so sorry for not being more sensitive. I'm still a blunt instrument, as you can see. Let's just start again and concentrate on the job we have to do. Your field trip is in a month and we have to do a lot of groundwork with your students. As always, they will be full of misconceptions about life in a South African township."

"Just so, Charlotte. Lots to do. So, come on. Let's get some lunch and start planning."

Matthew found himself retracing his steps to the Café Cam as though his path was mapped and rutted disallowing any deviance. Even the companionship of his *momentary-lover-in-time* failed to persuade him to explore new footsteps.

Arriving at the café, the now subdued and thoughtful couple seated themselves by the window to watch humanity drift by. They eyed the falafel and sushi before Matthew began an attempt to slice through the stiffness in the air that sat with them like a dystopian *ménage à trois*.

"Charlotte …."

"No, sorry, let me go first. I'm really sorry for that awkwardness a minute ago."

"Seriously. There is no need for apologies. I know I am an idiot."

"No, you are not. Look, what we had when you came over to Cape Town was really great. It really was. And if things were different then maybe we would have got it together. But the fact is that you were only there for a couple of weeks, so it had to be just what it was."

"Yes. I know that."

"The truth is, I really missed you when you went back. But I moved on. I moved on and I have got a really good boyfriend now. I think he might be the one."

"I'm very happy for you, Charlotte. I really am. I guess the truth is, that my life hasn't moved on."

"Don't be stupid. Of course you have moved on. I've been following your career. You have published loads. I understand there is another book on its way and you are up for professorship. At your age! A professorship! Christ, you are a shooting star!"

"Well, yes, my career is going well. But I meant that my *life* hasn't moved on."

"Oh, I see. So, no girlfriend then?"

"No girlfriend. No nothing. No change. Month by month; year by year; no change. No moving on since my divorce."

"Look, Matthew. I tell you what. We've got a job to do today, so how about we go out for a drink tonight and talk to each other as human beings instead of just talking shop?"

"Yes, I'd love that. But before we get started a quick word about that professorship thing. As you know, it's a tick box exercise. My publications are going well. I've discovered I can write a paper, then re-edit it for a chapter in my new book and then deliver it as a lecture. A triple whammy."

"So, you write it once and use it three times? Smart."

"Yup. But I still need to tick off some more keynotes. I'm not getting the numbers there. I did one for you in Cape Town, I've done one in Ottawa and I've even done one at John Hopkins."

"Yes, I know. Like I say, I've been watching your meteoric rise. I'm often quoting you in my stuff."

"Spare my blushes, Charlotte. Anyway, I've done loads around the UK too, but I need to get my international keynotes up if I'm going to hit the target for professorship. I don't suppose you've got anything for me, have you?"

"Well, I can defo offer you a keynote in a local conference at my Uni which is coming up. The dates fit OK with your visit; I think. But the University of the Western Cape is having its annual international conference later in August too. Do you want me to make a call to see if they have anything? One of their speakers has pulled out. I bet they'll bite your hand off."

Without waiting for a response, Charlotte punched her finger at her smart phone and a message shot its way to the University of the Western Cape.

"Thanks. Right, now, down to business. Let's order some grub. Shall we get a takeout and take it down by the river?"

"Yes, that's a good idea."

"They do a combo takeout. Sushi, falafel and shawarma."

"Perfect. Grab enough for two."

Matthew and Charlotte escorted their combo pack together with their inflated academic egos and Matthew's bruised self-being to the bank of the River Cam before engaging their palates and their combative, scholarly dialogue.

"So, Matthew. Ubuntu is the focus. What definitions do we start with?"

"Well, what I had in mind is that they should engage in some sort of interpretive research to explore the concept of ubuntu in Khayelitsha. You know, doing observations and interviews. That kind of stuff. Maybe a *learning walk* methodology. They need to collect a lot of data in a very short time. Then, when they get back, they have to apply their own understanding of ubuntu to Western European cultures. What do you think? I reckon that would give them masses of stuff for their assignments."

"Perfect. So, seminar number one – introduction and research methodologies. Seminar number two – perceptions of ubuntu."

"Sounds good. I think perhaps if I lead the research methodologies one since I have to mark their assignments and then you lead the ubuntu one. What do you think?"

"Yes. That works. But can we ask them to come prepared? Can we ask them to do some literature searches first? I don't want to lecture them on ubuntu. I'll want to have conversational style seminars."

"Exactly right. Can I ask you, as the specialist on ubuntu, where do you sit with it?"

"Right, well done, Matthew. You just hit the button. You really know how to get a girl going. Stand back, here we go."

Matthew sat back as ordered and switched on his mental Dictaphone.

"Well, we can always start with the Zulu perspective of ubuntu meaning *humanity.*"

"*I am because we are* or *I am because you are.*"

"Exactly. There'll be loads of discussion right there. Then we could go to the *universal bond of sharing that connects all humanity.*"

"I love it. Go on."

"We can obviously use the academic definitions, even if they are a bit dry, like, '*a collection of values and practices that people of Africa or of African origin view as making people authentic human beings.*"

"And then there is that Desmond Tutu quote. That's always a good one to use."

"Oh, yeah. *A person with ubuntu is open and available to others, affirming of others, does not feel threatened that others are able and good, based from a proper self-assurance that comes from knowing that he or she belongs in a greater whole and is diminished when others are humiliated or diminished, when others are tortured or oppressed.*"

"Wow. Impressive. Word for word."

"Of course. I can lecture about ubuntu in my sleep."

"I'm loving this, Charlotte."

"Me too, Matthew."

With barely pause for their eyes to meet and their lips to form smiles that might betray their affection and admiration for one another, the two academics fell into their safety zones and interrogated political, social and philosophical aspects of ubuntu. For a few hours they were connected by Nelson Mandela's thoughts, '*We are all bound together in ways that are invisible to the eye; that there is a oneness to humanity; that we achieve ourselves by sharing ourselves with others, and caring for those around us.*'

That evening Matthew and Charlotte met for drinks at the Anchor pub and sat on the terrace overlooking the River Cam in order to engage in non-academic conversation but inevitably fell into dialogue about potential future collaborations between St Michael's College and the University of Cape Town together with their subtler and more personal understandings of concepts of ubuntu. Later that night Charlotte fell into a deep sleep in the rooms provided for her and Matthew tapped on his laptop keyboard late into the early hours of the morning as the next chapter of his book found a coherence formulated by his now sleeping colleague and which would become amplified and expanded by the forthcoming seminars, the field trip and the submission of his students' assignments.

Ubuntu - implications for popular western cultures: a Socratic dialogue of perceptions and misperceptions.

September – Marianne

With his travel bag packed alongside his thoughts in readiness for his departure to Cape Town the following morning, Matthew found time to seek sanguinity on that bench on that green surrounded by a kaleidoscopic rainbow of dahlias and cleome. Another first day of another month felt timeless and illimitable.

His rumination of the impending visit to Cape Town was brutally interrupted by the appearance of a sturdy, middle-aged woman with startling, bleached hair and ruddy face. The abruptness with which she joined Matthew on *his* bench stirred his ire even before her assault on him had time to launch itself.

"What are you looking at?"

"Huh? What? Sorry?"

"You were staring at me. You perve."

"Perve? What? No, I was just sitting here?"

"It's not like I'm a Monday, or anything."

Matthew's instinct to run before getting dragged into something he felt intuitively would end in conflict was overridden by the reference to a person being described as a day of the week. He set aside his reticence as his academic curiosity propelled him through the looking glass and down into a deep, dark rabbit hole.

"A Monday? Sorry. I really don't understand."

"A Monday. Where have you been all your life? Nobody likes Mondays."

"Still not getting it. Is that some reference to, 'I don't like Mondays' by the Boomtown Rats?"

"What are you talking about? No, blacks. Nobody likes blacks."

"Jesus! What?"

"*Mondays*. Apparently, if I call them by the n-word I'm being a racist."

"Er, well, yeah. Using the n-word is totally racist. But if you are calling them Mondays, isn't that just as racist?"

"You calling me a racist? Christ. I sit down by a total stranger; he eyes me up and then the next thing I know he calls me a racist."

"I didn't eye you up and I don't think I called you a racist. I'm just confused by how you are using the *Mondays* thing."

"You thick or something?"

"Well, maybe, but I'm a lecturer here so maybe some think I'm quite smart."

"Oh, right you are one of those woke, lefties, aren't you?"

"This is going too fast for me. I'd really like to understand the *Monday* reference, but now you've just called me woke maybe you could explain that."

"Easy. But first things first. Perhaps we should introduce ourselves. You are?"

"Matthew. You?"

"Matthew the commie lecturer, eh? I'm Marianne."

"OK. Can I call you Mary?"

"Why? My name is Marianne."

"Sorry. Marianne it is. So, Marianne, you just called me woke. What do you mean by that?"

"You lot are always banging on about social justice and equality and stuff like that."

"OK, you are still going too fast for me. I'm still stuck on the *Monday* reference and now you are using the word *woke* like some sort of insult whilst defining it as a good thing and now you have just put me in some sort of *you lot* category. Seriously, I can't keep up."

"I bet you've got a million letters after your name but don't have two brain cells to rub together do you, Matthew?"

"Right. Another insult. Let's agree on that one then and go back to the beginning. *Mondays*. So, you are calling black and coloured people Mondays. Why?"

"I told you. Using the n-word makes me a racist."

"But using Mondays like you are using the n-word is just the same, isn't it?"

"If I use the n-word I'm a racist and if I call them Mondays I'm not. The fact is, I'm not a racist, but I think they should all go home and leave Britain to the British. I'm not racist because one of my friends is black."

"Really? What does he think of your views?"

"She actually. See, call yourself woke but you are a total sexist. You just assumed it was a *he*."

"Let's park the *he* or *she* thing for a minute. I'm still at the beginning of this conversation. Actually, I didn't call myself woke, you called me that. But if you mean I am aware of social issues around gender and race and that I believe in equality and mutual respect, then I can live with being accused of being woke. So, what does she think of your view that black people should all go home?"

"That's just a bunch of fancy words. Anyway, she is black and thinks all the immigrants should go home too. Britain used to be great, now it is overrun by immigrants. What's so wrong in wanting to get our country back. What's so wrong in making Britain great again?"

Matthew reeled as he heard the words that Trump and Brexit had driven into the consciousness of far-right populists. He knew he was battling irrational indoctrination in this conversation but he was drawn by the unfolding interpretation of cultural conflict.

"I'm still struggling to keep up. You keep making points and I never get to say my piece."

"Go on then. I'll shut up. I can't wait to hear what you have to say."

"Actually, I'd like to go back to your black friend. You say you are not a racist because she is black and that she agrees with your views about sending *them* back home. And by *them* I assume you mean black and coloured people." Matthew emphasised the word *them* to issue a challenge to Marianne.

"No, not just blacks and coloureds. All immigrants. All immigrants should go home and leave Britain to the British. She gets called a *coconut*. Bet you don't know what that means either."

"Actually, I think I do. Black on the outside and white on the inside. Right?"

"Yeah. You got one right at last."

"So does that imply that all white people are racist?"

"It's not racist to want your own country back."

"OK. I'm still struggling. Is your black friend an immigrant or was she born in the UK? Are you saying she is or isn't a racist? I'm just plain lost."

"God. Try to keep up. No wonder education is so crap in this country if people like you are in charge."

"Er, I'm not in charge of education. But look, that's another whole thing. Let's try to focus. Can we stay on the subject of racism?"

"You still calling me a racist?"

"Again, no. Actually. Let's cut to the quick. I'm off to South Africa tomorrow and I've got loads to do. OK, deep breath – yes, I think you are saying racist things. So yes, I think that makes you a racist, and yes, I'm calling you a racist."

"If by racist you mean I want the best for the people of this country and that others should go back to theirs and have the best for themselves in their country, then yes, I can live with being called a racist. See, I can do that too without having letters after my name."

"Marianne. I'm lost for words. There's no reasoning with you, is there?"

"If you had any valid points I'd listen, but you haven't actually made any points yet. You just see me as a racist because it suits your woke views. Just because I don't agree with you doesn't make me a racist. In fact, you lumping me together with racists makes you a racist, doesn't it?"

"Oh, Marianne. That's like saying my dog has four legs so that cat is a dog."

"Now you are just talking rubbish because you lost the argument. Anyway, you are off to South Africa? I reckon they had it right when the whites were in charge. It's all gone tits up now the blacks are running it. It isn't safe there now. I saw it on Facebook. The blacks are burning all the farms."

"Actually, Marianne, I saw that too, but it was just white supremacists' propaganda. Their videos were all just invented to push their racist agenda. I'm afraid you've been taken in."

"How do you know? Were you there?"

"Well not *there* exactly, but …"

"Well, how do you know, then?"

"Because it was investigated and found to be white supremacy crap." Matthew's voice had raised both in pitch and volume.

"Investigated by blacks, eh?"

"Well by the government actually."

"And who is president?"

"Matamela Cyril Ramaphosa."

"Out of interest, what colour is he?"

"Er, well, black."

"Proves my point, eh? Black man says black people are innocent and the white people are guilty. You decide that the blacks are telling the truth and that the whites are liars. Makes you the racist, eh?"

"Oh, come on, Marianne. I know I'm right and I also know I'm losing this argument."

"Right about what?"

"Oh, for heaven's sake! OK. Right. I'm going to say this and then run."

"I dare you."

"You, Marianne, have been indoctrinated by far-right, white supremacists by looking at stuff on social media to support your racist views. There, I said it."

"Oh my. A woke commie with balls. Whatever next? So, what you are saying is that what you look for to read makes you right and whatever I look for to read makes me wrong."

"Well, it's not quite ..."

"That's exactly what you said."

"Well, yes, I might have but ..."

"Struggling now, eh? At least you didn't run."

"True. That might be a mistake. Here we go, I'm going to have one last go. So, you say it should be Britain for the British. So, what about people of Pakistani origin, or Indian, or African or, for that matter anyone who was born and bred here even though their skin may be black or brown? Is Britain for them too?"

"Nope. They must have had coloured parents. They should all go home and leave Britain to the proper British."

"Proper British? What on earth does that mean?"

"British are white."

"What?"

"It's a fact. British are white."

"Sorry, Marianne. You are just the foulest racist I have ever come across. I'm going. Goodbye."

"That's it. Lose the argument and then run off crying to all your socialist mates."

"Socialist? What? Are you now saying that no socialists are racist?"

"Of course. Lefties are all woke."

"Oh, Marianne. Seriously I wish I could bottle you and drop you into some of my lectures. You wouldn't half stir things up. You are priceless."

"Right. I'm off. I'm done with teaching you. Last thing. Education. Education in this country is running us into the ground because of all the left wing, commie crap that you lot teach."

Matthew knew he should ignore the new gauntlet that Marianne had just slapped in his face but was unable to control his rising indignation.

"No, sorry, you are not getting away with that. We teach people to have open minds and not to follow the propaganda pumped out by fascists on social media."

"Oh, so now I'm a racist and a fascist?"

"You, Marianne, are a foul, white supremacist, fascist bigot."

Marianne paused, looked Matthew in the eye and concluded with icy cold words.

"Didn't like being wrong, did you? I always know when I've won because you lot just end up chucking insults because you don't have an argument. I'm off. Goodbye."

Marianne left Matthew dizzied and disorientated. Finally, he gathered himself and decided to head for the banks of the river Cam until he calmed down enough to head home to complete the final preparations for his field trip. Finding a space on the grass with a clear view of tourists attempting to master punting he sat down and closed his eyes in search of composure.

"Hello, Matthew? Are you stalking me now? Or are you just after round two?"

"Oh, shit. Marianne. I didn't see you."

"Well, that's nice. Did I remember you saying something about respecting each other or did I imagine it?"

"No, you are right. We should show respect. And I guess I have to be honest with myself, that makes me a total hypocrite because I don't respect you. I can't bring myself to respect you and your foul views."

"I noticed that, but the truth is you don't respect *me* because of my point of view."

Matthew opened his eyes wide as her words hit his academic armour like a guided missile.

"Marianne, you are right. I'm sorry. I do not respect your views and that made me disrespect you as a person. I apologise. It made me angry and I resorted to personal abuse. My behaviour was indefensible. But you have to admit that it is hard to separate out a person's views from the person."

"Is that it? Is that all you've got?"

"Er, I think so."

"Well, I think I also seem to remember you banging on about teaching open mindedness? Well, I'm not sure you are open minded. According to you, your view is right and anyone who has a different view is wrong."

"Touché, Marianne. But surely you are not saying you are open minded?"

"Oh, no. I'm a full-on racist. I actually know it and I'm proud of it. I was messing with you. I rather enjoyed seeing you fall apart."

"Hum. I think I just found some respect for you. You totally played me, didn't you? And won."

"Anyway. I mean it. Every country should be filled with its own people and we should then respect each other. Like you say, Matthew, we should respect each other. Nothing wrong in respecting other people as long as they stay in their own country."

"Marianne. I disagree, but I respect your view. I respect you as a person for sticking to your view."

"You are just saying that now because you don't have any arguments left."

"No, I mean it. You taught me an important lesson. In a global society we must listen to and respect others' views whilst separating the person from the view."

"You are so smart and yet know so little, Matthew."

"You are not the first person to say that."

"Why am I not surprised?"

"Again, touché. Look, I'm off to South Africa tomorrow. A country which was once occupied by its black, indigenous peoples and then got invaded by white people. Invaded rather a lot actually. So, who do you think should live there now? Blacks or white? Or should they live in harmony with each other?"

"Dunno, Matthew. I'm only bothered about my own country. You are the smart one, remember? You figure it out."

"I wish I could."

"There's one thing I'm sure of though. You'll be siding with the blacks whilst you are out there. Do you know why?"

"Go on, tell me."

"Because you are a prejudiced racist."

"Oh, dear God, Marianne. I can't tell you how much I want to disagree with you, but I can't."

"Maybe I should get a job lecturing at your college, then."

"Please don't Marianne."

"Why? Which college is it?"

"St Michael's."

"Ah, that's the one with a statue of Tobias Charleston outside its front door, isn't it?"

"Yes, it is, and I can see where you are going here. I may as well give up now."

"Yes, Matthew, Charleston the slave trader. Look, I get that because I think white people should be left alone to live in their own country makes me a racist, well, I can live with that, but slavery? Seriously? Slavery in any form is shit. So, Matthew, don't you lecture me. At least I'm honest about what I believe in and what I am? Can you say that?"

"Marianne, I am so clever but I sometimes don't even know who I am."

"No, worries, Matthew. I'm pleased to have helped you."

"You have. I mean it. You have really helped me, but I honestly have to go now. I'd love to say I hope we meet again, but I would be lying."

"Don't worry, the feeling is mutual. Tell you what. I'm at a Britain First rally in London, in a month. Come along and I'll continue your education."

"You won't be surprised when I tell you that there is no way on earth that I'll be going on a Britain First rally. But, and I genuinely mean it, I do respect you."

"Then my work is done. Have a good trip. Send my regards to all the *Mondays* in South Africa. Tell them to stay there."

All Matthew found was a grin to acknowledge her final, well aimed mortar. With a nod he rose and headed back to his laptop. This chapter did not fall easily from his fingers. This chapter explored his encounter with Marianne, but in reality, explored his own prejudices. The long-haul flight he was about to endure would similarly torture him as he tried to reconcile that he was about to lead a trip to a township filled with black people subjugated by whites. Moreover, he and his white colleagues were about to lead a group of white students in researching the predominately black paradigm of ubuntu. *"Still, masses of material there. Maybe I can use some of it into my keynote."*

The shape of his next academic treatise began.

The role of social media platforms in the rise of populist counter-culture in western Europe: Lessons to be learned

October – Helena

Matthew's return from his field trip inevitably found him in deep thought reflecting on his recent experiences in Khayelitsha. He had immersed himself if their culture and embraced their sense of being. He had shared food and drink with them and had joined the many street singing groups whose harmonies had burrowed into his soul. His newly emerging self-interrogation had challenged his apperception of both himself and his relationship with his normalcy. As he sat on that familiar bench on that familiar green in his home town of Cambridge even the scent and raucous chromaticity of the alstroemeria and nerines failed to penetrate his darkening thoughts. His field trip had been an unmitigated success. His keynote speech at the international conference at the University of the Western Cape had been a triumph and had drawn two more invitations to speak at conferences in Washington DC and Perth. He could even admit that he had enjoyed the company of Charlotte and her now fiancé as well as the incessant flirtatiousness of Kayla. Achieving professorship looked even more likely than ever and would draw him into a web of high expectations and narrow focus. Somehow his successes in academia underlined the failure in his personal life. Success in one in no way mitigated failure in the other.

The blueness of the opalescent, cumulus-laden sky above him failed to penetrate the dark clouds subsuming his self-worth. He felt his guts clenching and his chest tightening as another year was proving itself to be unvaried from the preceding years. His arms autonomously wrapped themselves around his torso and his eyes shut tight to deny the pressure building behind them. He had earned academic success by his relentless focus but had failed in life effortlessly.

Softly spoken words found recognition in his consciousness as they bathed his awareness and beckoned to be allowed entry into the moment in time he was using to pity himself.

"Are you OK?"

His reticent response was to raise his vision to meet a pair of dark brown eyes which bore a softness matched by the voice of their owner. Words escaped him and the stranger repeated her inquiry.

"Are you OK? I don't want to interfere, but I just wondered if you are alright."

"Yes, I'm good. Honestly."

"Are you sure, you were looking a bit troubled."

"Yes, I'm fine. Or at least I will be."

"What do you mean, *will be*?"

"Oh, nothing. Sorry. I'm being melodramatic."

"Do you want to talk? I know I'm a stranger, but talking can help. Talking to a stranger can sometimes help."

"No, I'm OK. Really."

"I'm Helena. I'll leave you to it, if you are sure."

"I'm Matthew. Yeah. I'm fine. But thanks, anyway."

"OK, Matthew. Just one thing before I go."

Helena reached into her modestly decorated shoulder bag, drew out a folded paper and handed what appeared to be a small flyer to Matthew.

"It's fine if you don't want to talk to me, but maybe you just might want to talk to God. He can be a great comfort."

Out of politeness rather than inquisitiveness Matthew extended his hand to receive the unwanted gift as he offered her a consolatory smile.

"Sorry, Helena, but God isn't for me. But thanks, anyway."

"I know."

"Huh? What do you mean by that?"

"You are Dr Matthew Huxley, aren't you?"

"Er, yes. I am. Have we met before? Sorry, I'm terrible with faces."

"Not met exactly. Do you remember doing a guest lecture a couple of years ago at the Cambridge Institute for Continuing Education? Well, I was in the audience. I remember your lecture really well."

"Wow. It must have been a good one. My students only remember my lectures long enough for them to pass their assessments. What was the context?"

"You were arguing against the existence of God."

"Oh, yeah, I remember. I remember it going down like a lead balloon. No-one felt it necessary to tell me I was talking to a room full of born-again evangelists."

"No, Matthew, it was really good. Honestly. I really enjoyed it. True, I might have been the only one in the room who did enjoy it. I don't think you made many friends that day."

"Well, if you are pushing God-leaflets at strangers, I guess I didn't persuade you that God can't possibly exist."

"Of course you didn't change my mind, because God exists in my heart. The fact that you can't see him doesn't make his existence any less real to me. God is in my heart and no argument you could ever make can change that."

"Sure. Seriously, Helena, do want this conversation?"

"Of course I do. If you don't mind being proved wrong."

Matthew's academic ire was again raised as he knew he was about to engage in battle, but it was to be a battle that he knew he would win.

"OK. Let's do it, then. Where shall we start, Helena?"

"You start, Matthew. I'm guessing an academic like you is all too familiar with my arguments so you tell me where you are coming from."

"OK. Here it is. I'm an atheist. I'm a humanist. I believe in a paradigm of good and a paradigm of bad but I can't accept the iconifying of the paradigms and I definitely can't accept some sort of imaginary deity watching over me in judgment. I am an individual with free thought and I am responsible for what I do and what I say. I have to be responsible for the consequences of my words and actions."

"Wow. When I said start you really went all the way."

"Sorry."

"Actually, I reckon that was a pretty good summary of your hour-long lecture."

Matthew was disarmed enough by Helena's flippancy to allow his guard to slip sufficiently for him to give his new adversary licence to respond.

"Right, Helena. Your turn. Shall we start with monotheism - *One God*?"

I'll go anyway you want with this. Yes, Matthew, *One God*. *One God* who is within you. We each have *One God*. Our own God. It doesn't matter what we call him, or her, or it. Our God is ours and so it is the one and only God each of us have."

"When you say we each have a *One God*, I have to disappoint you – I don't. Do you know how many Gods there are? The truth is, I've lost count. Do we start with Greek mythology? Maybe start with Zeus, the most powerful God in Greek mythology. Or perhaps Odin from Nordic religion? Or how about Celtic Gods? It goes on and on. Let's say there have been more than a billion people on the planet, shall we. If they each had their own God, like you say, then there are more than a billion Gods. The bottom line is, that I'm not one of those with a one God. So, do I disappoint you?"

"Yes, you do."

"Explain!"

"Well, you said it yourself. You believe in a paradigm of good. That's your God. You can call it what you want and you don't have to go to church."

"Ah, there's a difference. I don't iconify the paradigm and I don't worship it."

"Who said you have to. We are just the same. We both believe in a paradigm of good. I call mine God as a sort of shorthand."

"Well, I'm not sure you are typical. Most Christians worship God as an icon."

"You are wrong there, Matthew. Most Christians understand the difference between the icon and purpose. Of course, there are extremists and there are fundamentalists, but they are not typical."

"OK, what else have you got?"

"Well, that thing you said about an imaginary deity sitting in judgement. What if I just call it my conscience. My conscience which is being guided by the paradigms of good and bad which inform my moral compass? Then aren't we just the same again?"

"Well, I guess so. But I still don't believe in God."

"Fair enough. Let's agree to disagree then, apart from the fact we've agreed on just about everything so far."

"No. No. I don't believe in God. End of."

"End of? A bit final, eh? Not a very coherent argument, is it?"

"Sorry. I didn't mean to be rude. Look, everyone knows the church is only there historically to collect taxes and to control the serfs. The populous were told to pay their taxes to the church or face eternal damnation. Then there's all the religious wars. Millions of people slaughtered arguing over who has the most peaceful God."

"Matthew. Simplistic, sweeping statements. That's not worthy of you. Again, I'll not disagree, except that you are describing people not God. There are bad people in the world but that doesn't prove God doesn't exist. People have free will. You said that yourself. So, you have to expect there to be good people and bad people. People who will use their God as an excuse to justify their own evil."

"OK. Then church, let's do the church thing. People go to church with a social agenda and a belief in God is just an excuse for a get-together. Then they pray for an end to poverty before bunging a fiver in the collection and going home for a roast dinner."

"Again, I can't disagree. But churches play a really important role in the cohesion of society. If people benefit by getting together to share their concerns for one another and for humanity, then I reckon churches are a good thing. It is an opportunity for people to share their paradigms of good. It helps them direct their moral compass."

"Well, maybe, but …."

"So, Matthew, where next? The ontological argument, or maybe the causal argument, then perhaps the modern design argument or maybe the anthropic cosmological principle and not forgetting the experiential and pragmatic arguments."

"Helena. Who the hell are you? I wasn't expecting you to start being rational. I thought you were just going to stuff God down my throat and then damn me to your imaginary hell as a heretic for not agreeing with you. I really, really don't believe in God."

"Well, full disclosure, then. I'm Professor Helena Madden. I'm Professor of Divinity at Lincoln College in Oxford."

"Bloody hell, you might have said."

"Where would the fun have been in that?"

"I made a total fool of myself, didn't I?"

"Not at all, but you were so easy. I did have a bit of an advantage. I heard your lecture so I knew where you would go. Plus, I caught you off-guard. Demolishing you was easy. Have you read any of my stuff?"

"I can't say I have. But what is an Oxford Professor of Divinity doing stuffing God propaganda leaflets into the hands of strangers in Cambridge?"

"Ah, that. That was a bit of a gamble. I reckoned you'd be cocky enough not to look at it."

Matthew reluctantly looked down at the crumpled paper in his hand.

"Well played, Helena. It's a flyer for your book signing this afternoon at Heffer's Bookshop. *The God Collective. Worshiping the ideal.* Clever. Clever book title and clever you stuffing the flyer in my hand. You totally got me. I am so arrogant I thought I knew what the flyer was and I thought I could outsmart you. I fell at every single hurdle."

"If only I had a conscience, Matthew, I might feel guilty leading you into my trap, but the truth is, I'm an academic so point scoring with another academic comes naturally."

"Well, on that, we agree totally. Ten nil to you at least. I'm usually better at it myself. I'll be ready for you next time. You'll find me a worthy opponent."

"Tell you what, if you come to my signing this afternoon Matthew, I'll give you a freebie. My book sets out the argument for one God being everyone's *good*. Why don't you read it and then we'll have another discussion?"

"OK. Challenge accepted. Very clever premise too, by the way."

"Thanks. In fact, Matthew. When you're ready after you've read it, I'll send you an invite to Oxford and you and I can have a Socratic dialogue with my students. I'll argue for the existence of God, you can argue against and then we'll invite the students to cross-question us. I've got a gap in my course schedule in a month so maybe you could fill that for me."

"I'm not sure I'd survive. Sounds like you are inviting me into the lions' den."

"Oh, I think you'll rise to it. Actually, I think you already have."

"Hum. You might be right. To be honest, I could do with something new to get my teeth into. Challenge accepted. Then I'll invite you back here for round two."

"Accepted. This'll be fun."

"How long are you here for?"

"Just today. My publisher is stumping up enough cash for one day for the signing. I'm back off to Oxford first thing tomorrow."

"Fancy joining me for dinner after your signing?"

"Actually, Matthew, that would be great. I'm on expenses, so you choose where and then it'll be my treat."

"Deal. I'll book Restaurant 22. It's a great place and costs a fortune – that'll be payback for your deception. I'll see you for the signing then."

"Great. Meanwhile, do you fancy a stroll along the Cam? It'll give me an opportunity to apologise for ambushing you."

"Yes. Let's pick up a coffee at the Café Cam and take a stroll. They do a nice line in sushi too if you fancy a picnic. We may as well make the most of the last of the summer."

"Coffee is great, but I have a lunch date with my publisher."

"OK, coffee it is. If you are getting the most expensive dinner in Cambridge this evening then I'll treat you to a coffee."

Laughter cemented their bond and Matthew and Helena rose, strolled over the bridge to collect their caffeinated takeaways and shared a slow-motion engagement as equals before Helena left to meet her publishers for lunch prior to her book signing at Heffer's book shop later that day and before meeting Matthew for dinner.

Matthew spent a few minutes alone collecting his thoughts ready to pick Helena's undoubtedly brilliant mind over dinner in order to begin populating the next chapter of his book which would inevitably take him deep into the night. Reading her book would both give him prose to quote her in his writings but most importantly the process would prepare his arguments for the academic combat he had accepted.

Religions, faiths and churches: their roles in sociocultural ontogenesis

November – Michelle

Sitting on that bench on that green on the first day of another month chilled Matthew's soul. The cold air, grey skies and leaf carpet drew him towards a feeling that had become all too familiar. The greyness of the sky bore down on him greying his inner being. The floral displays which had raised his spirits as the months of the year rolled by had surrendered to brown wood chippings now sealing and protecting the flower beds ready for their winter slumber.

Matthew pulled his fleece lined coat around him and sunk his hands into its deep pockets to protect his darkening mood.

Ready for the warmth of coffee he raised himself up onto his feet and rounded his shoulders ready to retrace his steps to the Café Cam. His eyes immediately engaged those of a young girl. Maybe early twenties, he thought. Attractive, but unkempt. Her shoes were worn and a broken backpack threatened to spill its contents through a tear in its side. Her eyes fixed his and Matthew found himself drawn to a tale yet unspoken.

"Sorry to disturb you, Sir. Can you spare some change?"

Matthew knew that giving money would seldom contribute to solving the underlying problems of what he assumed to be a homeless person, but he could not tear his attention from the sadness and beauty of the broken being in front of him.

"You don't need to call me Sir. I'm Matthew."

"I'm Michelle. I just want a coffee. I'm so cold. If you have any spare change it would help."

Compassion raced through Matthew like a rapier. He already knew he would buy her breakfast and so searched for words to lessen the charitable impact on this young person's self-worth should he find the fortitude to make the offer of more than just coffee.

"I'll buy you a coffee. I was just going to get one anyway. Look, there is a café just round the corner. The Café Cam – it's my regular. They do nice food there. Come with me and I'll buy you breakfast."

"No, sorry, Sir. Er, Matthew. I know that café. They take one look at me and tell me to leave. They won't let me in."

"I'm one of their best customers. They'll let us in."

"No, I can't stand the way they look at me. I'm sorry to have bothered you. Have a good day, Matthew."

Addressing him as Matthew again tugged at his benevolence.

"OK. Wait. Tell you what. Would it be OK if I grabbed a couple of coffees and maybe a bacon roll or something? I'll bring them back here. There's another café down the road that does great breakfast baps. Maybe we could talk for a bit."

"You don't need to do that, Sir."

Hearing the title, Sir, steeled his intent.

"Matthew. I'm Matthew. And no, I know I don't have to but I want to. And just to be clear, I'm not trying to chat you up or hit on you or take advantage or anything. I really was just going to get myself a coffee. It's up to you. I don't want to make you feel awkward or anything. Coffee and bacon bap. You decide. Yes, or no?"

"Thank you. Yes, that would be very kind of you. Can I wait here?"

"Yes, of course. Keep my seat warm. Oh, that wasn't very tactful, was it? Yes. Just wait here. I'll be ten minutes."

Laden with a bag full of sandwiches, two bacon baps and two large coffees, Matthew's heart raised and then fell as he returned to that bench, now empty, on that green. He found himself scanning the Cambridge landscape for signs of Michelle. Locating a bowed body sitting on a bench almost out of view further along the River Cam, Matthew strode cautiously to seek his new companion. On reaching the bench, Michelle looked up and eyed the bag of food and coffees.

"You don't need to do this, Matthew. I moved. Sorry. I didn't really expect you to come back."

"No, I know. Look, I've got coffees, bacon baps and a bagful of sandwiches for you. I know I'm crossing a line here, but I don't care. Look. I'll just leave it here for you if you want. I won't intrude. But I'd really like to sit with you for a while if that's OK with you."

"Matthew, I'm very grateful. Seriously. But you don't have to sit with me. I'm not your problem."

"Are you a problem?"

"I don't want to be."

"Then no, you are not my problem. You are not a problem to me. So, with your permission, I'll sit here a while and we'll have breakfast together."

"You are a kind man, Matthew. Most people just look away when they see me."

Matthew accepted her words as an invitation and sat on the polar end of the bench to Michelle, placed the bag of food between them and handed her a coffee.

"I hate this time of year," said Matthew hoping to find a way into a conversation.

"Me too."

Silence hovered as Michelle gripped the paper cup with both hands and gulped the hotness of the coffee into her chilled soul.

Matthew swallowed the silence in order to provoke his soulful companion but eventually offered words intended to draw his new acquaintance into discourse.

"If I told you that I hated this time of year because I find it so boring and I don't really like Christmas and New Year, I bet you'd hate me."

"Of course I don't hate you. I expect we hate this time of year for different reasons. For me, it's the cold. The wet. The pointlessness of it all."

"Are you sleeping rough, Michelle?"

"Yes."

"It's none of my business, but isn't there anywhere for you to go? A hostel or something?"

"Hostels and stuff? Yes, but I hate it there. I've tried and tried, but I just can't sleep in those places. So, I sleep outside. I try to hide. It's a bit scary on my own."

"I bet. Or rather, I can't even begin to imagine. So, Michelle, tell me to mind my own business, but how did you end up on the streets?"

"Don't worry, I'm not a junkie or a prostitute or anything. And I'm definitely not dangerous."

"I promise, I wasn't making any assumptions. I know enough to know it can be complicated. I know enough to understand that every story is different. So, what happened to make you homeless? I should apologise again. I have a habit of analysing everything. I just blurt questions out before I think of their impact on people. I'm a bit of a dork, if truth be told."

"Don't worry. This is the longest conversation I've had for months."

Michelle broke abruptly from conversation and embraced the smell, taste and luxury of the bacon bap. Matthew joined her in genuine solidarity.

After completing her gustatory comradeship, Michelle folded her arms and tucked her hands into her armpits to protect them from the cold.

"So, Matthew. What is this going to cost me?"

"What? No. I don't expect anything."

"Really?"

"You are not suggesting I'm suddenly going to molest you, are you? I promise. I'm not like that."

"No, I trust you. I've learned who to trust and who to run from. So, what is it you want, then? And don't lie. I sense it."

"Well, I guess you might be right, but I hadn't realised it. I hadn't meant it. The fact is, I'm a lecturer at a Cambridge college. I lecture in anthropology. I keep finding myself meeting people and then I end up analysing them. It's a really bad habit. Makes me a bit sad, eh? But that isn't why I offered to buy you breakfast. Seriously, I was just trying to be kind. But then I just sort of got hooked in and found myself wanting to understand."

"Wow. That's refreshing."

"What?"

"Someone being honest with me. I'm used to being ignored, patronised, shouted at and vilified. Honesty is a rare commodity out here on the streets. Alright, Matthew, if you want my story, you've got it."

"Are you sure? I don't want to be a pain. Tell you what, why don't you come back to my place and we can talk in the warm. Again, that's not a line to take advantage of you. It is just that it is bloody freezing today."

"Thanks, but no thanks. I'd feel awkward. Besides, if I tell you my story out here, maybe the cold will make it more real for you."

"OK. Good point. Tell me whatever you want to say. I'll try not to interrupt with questions, but I know myself, I'll probably butt in all the time."

"I like you, Matthew. So, here goes. I was in the army. I served in Iraq. I was there after the war. Even after the papers stopped reporting on it, there was plenty of fighting. It went on for years. I was sent there after my training in 2015. Me and a bunch of mates. It was all OK for a while. Then, one day, we were heading between camps in a truck. We hit a landmine. It blew us to kingdom come and back. I was lucky, so they say. I got out alive. My mates were blown to bits."

"Jesus!"

"Yeah. It was shit. Look, I'm not going to aim for the bleeding hearts story. Fact is, I was given tons of support and eventually I was prepared for civilian life. I got as much support as I needed. I got a job. Oh, I should have said, I was a nurse. Anyway, I got a job in a hospital, got a flat and basically had a pretty good life."

"So, what went wrong?"

"Then it started. About two years after I left. Full-on PTSD."

"Post-traumatic stress disorder?"

"Yes. It took over my life. I couldn't sleep, I couldn't eat. I had panic attacks. Dreadful nightmares. It just took my life away. It took my mates away too. They didn't know how to handle it, so they drifted away one by one. I called the Samaritans about ten times a day, but even that got pretty samey. I call them Robo-Sams. They'd just kept asking me how I felt and eventually I got tired of being asked the same questions and of giving the same answers."

"But didn't the army keep supporting you? The hospital where you worked? Therapy? I dunno. You tell me."

"Oh, yes. I was in a very caring profession. They really did a job on me, but bit by bit I fell apart. My so-called friends had already gone. I can't blame them. Well, to cut a long story short, I couldn't cope. I resigned my job, lost my flat and ended up out here. I tried all sorts of hostels. They just didn't work for me. Then it just becomes a self-fulfilling prophecy. Now I'm homeless and living on the streets, begging for coffees. So, I'm in no place to get a job or anything. I just live from day to day. I'm in a spiral I can't get out of. It's the classic catch twenty-two. I'm on the streets because I don't have a job and I can't get a job because I'm on the streets."

"Michelle. That's horrible, but I guess your story is all too common."

"Not really. There are thousands of us vets living rough. But please don't think I'm typical or something. Talk to any one of them and you'll get a different story."

"I don't know what to say, Michelle. But what about all the support available? Government, local authorities, charities – there must be lots of support, surely."

"Oh, yes. I'm not complaining. Not really. It's me. My brain is so fried I just can't get into the space where I can take advantage of it."

"Michelle, I really want to help. What can I do?"

"For a college lecturer you're not that bright, are you?"

"Oh, so many people keep telling me that."

"You are missing the point. You can't do anything. Only I can. I need to sort my head out before anyone can do anything. That's the problem."

"But surely there is something I can do."

"You have. You listened to me."

"I meant something more tangible."

"Again, Matthew, I'm not your problem. I know that I am a problem. I know people look at me and assume I'm some sort of down and out drug addict. Someone to be swept off the streets so I can't be seen. Oh, I know I'm a problem, but most of all, I'm a problem to myself."

"Can't I do something to break the cycle? I'd really like to get you back on your feet. If I could do something ..."

"I know you mean well, but no, there is nothing you can do. I wish it was that easy. Here's something that might amuse you. Sometimes when I'm sleeping out, police make up charges to arrest me."

"Christ, that's terrible."

"No, you don't get it. It's the young police mostly. They make up charges so they can arrest me and put me in a cell for the night. They do it to give me shelter and food just for a night. They do it out of compassion. The older police are more heartless."

Matthew sat, body and soul chilled to the core unable to find words and sentences to express his genuine wish to offer help.

"There must be something I can do. Please help me out here."

"OK, Matthew, there might be something. There's a church in Cambridge - St Mary's I think - they are doing a fundraiser in a month to get money ready for a Christmas dinner they provide for us tramps. Why don't you help out there? Maybe I'll see you for Christmas dinner."

"Michelle. It's a date. I promise. I'll be there. Now, you've got to promise me that you'll be there too. Promise?"

"I promise. I'll look forward to it, Matthew."

Michelle rose and bowed deferentially.

"Thanks again. Thanks for the coffee but mostly for the company. Thank you for listening. It meant a lot. It really helped."

"No worries. Don't forget your bag of sandwiches."

"Thanks again."

"And if you see me just come over. I mean it. I ... I ..."

"Yes. I will. Thanks again. See you on Christmas day, Matthew."

"You will."

Matthew was left alone, his thoughts of Michelle now overshadowing his own darkness. He knew another chapter beckoned but also knew it would take endless research to unravel. He mentally earmarked Rosa as a new student in search of a research focus who might be well placed to undertake the research task for him. Even so, the skeleton of the next chapter in his book began forming itself. He knew he would be writing from the heart with little care for what the inevitable judgement academic scrutiny would heap on him.

As he typed relentlessly into the night, the lyrics to *Homeless* by Ladysmith Black Mambazo aided his disquietude and drew ubuntu into conflict with Michelle's plight.

Seeing the unseen and ending the spiral: Motivating military veterans to accept support

December – Sally

Early snow threatened that bench on that green whilst Matthew sat, swaddling himself in his now worn, fleece-lined winter coat. His woollen hat and his thermal gloves made a gallant effort to hold back the frost which was beginning to recede in response to the temperature slowly climbing its way above freezing and as the watery sun began threatening to make an appearance. Another first day of another month annotated itself as: *the last first day of the last month of another year*. A year in which, Matthew considered had taken him on an unexpected journey and which had challenged his self-perceptions. Before his self-analysis wound itself into self-interrogation, or worse, self-pity, a familiar and affectionate figure planted itself alongside him, leaned over and kissed him on his cheek.

"Sally! Hi. Long-time-no-see."

Matthew's words felt more sincere than he had intended. A day seldom ended without thoughts of Sally but she had moved on and left him behind. Since their divorce, they had continued living in the same city but had seldom seen each other. A fact, Matthew thought, which underlined how far apart they must have drifted even before their mutual parting.

"How are you doing, Matthew? I see you are still living on the same bench on the same green."

"Neat first barbed comment, Sally."

"Oh, come on, Matthew. Joking. I was just joking. I thought we'd moved on. I thought we were at least civil with each other. I actually thought we were still friends. Not BFFs maybe, but friends nonetheless."

"Yes, Sally. We are. Sorry. I didn't mean to be brusque. As you see, my social skills are still pretty much nil."

"Yup. You always had the knack of saying exactly the right thing to an academic audience and totally the wrong thing socially."

"Nothing has changed there. My social life is crap, but my academic life is going well. I'm actually up for professorship. I thought it might be this year, but I think it'll be next year now. Apparently, I need to work on my *business case*."

"Business case! It's not like starting a business, is it? It's not like you are going to be selling bikes or something."

"Actually, Sally, it is just like that. I'm a commodity. The university will pimp me out, sell my publications and make loads of money out of me."

"Bloody hell. I knew academia was mercenary, but that's nuts. Are you sure you want that?"

"Welcome to my world, Sally. No, if I'm honest. I'm doubting my career plan. I'm having a bit of a personal crisis actually. Anyway Sally, changing the subject, I see you are fat."

"Well spotted and very nicely phrased, if I may say so? Yes, I'm pregnant. I'm due in a month. She'll be a New Year baby."

"Congratulations, Sally. Seriously. I'm stoked for you. I know you wanted a family. It was one of the many things I didn't give you."

"Now, don't start. We were good when we were good. We did the right thing going our separate ways when we did. It's a shame we had to go through the divorce. You know, Matthew, sometimes I think about it. If we had just lived together rather than get married, we wouldn't have had to get divorced. The word divorce summons up such ugliness. But I don't regret the time we had together."

"Nor me. Sometimes I wish we could have stayed together, but I know we are better off apart. You seem to be doing well, Sally."

"I've never been happier, Matt. Simon's business is doing well, I'm able to work from home and there's a baby on her way. Right now, I'm as happy as I could be. I'd not change anything."

"I'm happy for you, Sally. Genuinely."

"And you? The grapevine hasn't been too forthcoming. Apart from probably becoming one of the youngest professors in the land, what have you been up to?"

"Same old. Work is going well. Student numbers are up. I've been doing some international work. I've been to Cape Town again. My new book is nearing completion and … well, that's it really."

"No new lady in your life?"

"Nope."

"Really? Matthew, you are a catch. Sort of fairly OK looking. Too smart for your own good. What's not to like?"

"You have such a nice way with words."

"No, seriously. You are good looking, successful and you have a heart bigger than a planet. Anyone would be lucky to have you. I mean it. Anyone but me, obviously."

"Obviously. No, no-one on the horizon. To be honest, I've met a bunch of new people this year. I actually thought one of them might be it. But I guess they all saw through me and I just repelled them all. If there is one thing I'm good at, it's driving women away."

"Now, come on, Matthew. Don't go all morose on me. Actually, one of my friends is on the market. She's good looking, nice tits, fairly smart. How about I set you up?"

"Er, have I got this right? My ex is trying to set me up with a someone who is fairly smart and has nice tits? Bit weird."

"Well, I was joking about the tits. Come on, Matthew, where is your sense of humour?"

"Sorry. I'm feeling a bit stuck in life."

"Right my little grumps. I don't believe you. There must be something you are looking forward to."

"Well, maybe. There is something. But until you asked, I hadn't realised it."

"Great, spill the beans. What is it?"

"OK. But don't fall off the bench when I tell you. It wouldn't do you any good in your condition. The fact is, I'm not going to my parents' house for Christmas."

"Oh, Matthew. You rebel. You have turned into a heretic! So, *not* going to your parents is something to look forward to. What did your parents say?"

"Hum. I didn't think about that. I'm going to have to tell them, aren't I?"

"I think a mention might be in order. I think they'd spot the empty chair at the dinner table if you just didn't turn up. So, anyway, what are you doing for Christmas? Off skiing? Seeking enlightenment in the Andes? Spill the beans. Lowen and I are all ears?"

"Lowen?"

"Lowen. She who is yet to be born. Lowen is Cornish for *joyful*. Did I mention we have a holiday home in Padstow?"

"You have now. I'm a bit jealous of that, if I'm honest. We had some great holidays in Cornwall, didn't we?"

"Yeah. Some of my happiest memories with you, Matt. You can use it any time. I mean it. It's at your disposal. Anyway, I'm still on the edge of my seat. What are you doing for Christmas?"

"I'm serving Christmas dinner to homeless people at St Mary's."

"What? Seriously? That's new. You were always, well, so self-absorbed. No offence."

"None taken. I know. It surprised me too. I've had a few Damascus moments this year."

"Wow. And there's you trying to make me believe nothing has changed. Maybe not much has changed in your life, but *you* have changed. And isn't that what really matters?"

"Oh, Sally. Wise words from you. I guess you have changed too on that front."

"Guilty as charged. Simon has been good for me. I'm not quite the bimbo I was. I guess we have both grown."

"Maybe we needed to be apart to find ourselves, eh, Sally?"

"I agree. As I say. I have no regrets. We were good together and better apart."

"We've finally found something we agree on. Are you in a rush, or do you fancy a coffee?"

"Coffee would be great. Let me guess. Café Cam?"

"Café Cam. One day I might try another café just to be daring."

"Time to start your education, Matt. Come with me. I'm taking you to the Punt Inn for coffee. Let's see if you can stand the shock of going to a new café."

"OK. I'm up for living dangerously. Let's go. My treat."

"Actually, I've got a favour to ask, but let's get coffee first. I'm starving too. I'm eating for two, or at least that's my excuse."

Sally picked up the pace with her long strides and Matthew followed as they wove their way through the throngs of students and tourists. Matthew caught a glimpse of a mobility scooter pausing at a doorway and Rosa leaning downwards to place coins in a paper cup being cradled by Michelle. It was that image that followed Matthew as Sally paused at regular intervals to embrace, kiss and converse with numerous friends. Her verbosity left Matthew dumb with envy. He had always admired Sally's ability to show genuine comradery and to converse on any topic with consummate ease.

Finally arriving at the Punt Inn for coffee, Sally breezed in and was greeted with faux affection by the owner. She quickly chose a table by the window overlooking the café's private mooring on the River Cam. There, they watched the café's punt, bearing the name *Espresso,* bob lazily in the wake of a passing rowing boat whilst mindfully exploring where to begin their conversation.

"Well, Matthew. Some things haven't changed, have they? You still leave all the talking up to me, don't you?"

"It would have been nice to get a word in edgeways, Sally."

Sally's stare froze Matthew as he grappled to find an apology which he demonstrably failed to do.

"Here we go again, eh, Matthew? Let's stop this. Truce?"

"Truce. I'm sorry."

"No more sorries."

"No more sorries. No more fighting. There's no point."

"Agreed. I don't want to fight. Truth is, Matthew, I still hold a very special place for you in my heart."

"Me too."

"So, anyway. This is what I want to ask you. After little baby Lowen makes her appearance, I'd really like you to be her Godfather."

"Bloody hell, Sally. I wasn't expecting that. Do you mean it?"

"Totally. Simon and I have discussed it. I think you still like him deep down. Honestly. He's a nice guy. Anyway. We are going for the Christening option and we'd like you to be Godfather. What do you think?"

"I don't know what to say? You know I'm not religious, don't you?"

"Yeah. I don't think it matters. Well, not if we don't tell anyone."

"Well …."

"That's a 'no', isn't it? I know you well enough to read you."

"Yes, it's a no. I was stalling to try to find an excuse. But I don't have an excuse. I do have a reason, though. I'm really sorry, but if you want Lowen to have a Godfather I really think you need someone who can do the whole God thing. I can't do that. I'd be a hypocrite if I said yes."

"OK. Man of principle, as always, Matthew. I was ready for that too. So, I have a plan 'B'. We are going for the

Christening, mainly to please Simon's parents. However, what if you just treated it like an atheist naming-ceremony. Then we can cite you as a secular 'Guardian'. The truth is, if we lived together, I think we'd kill each other, but I do still care about you. If I'm really, really honest, I may just still love you a little bit. I know we didn't have kids, but I'd still like you to be a part of my life and be a part of Lowen's. And, not to be too morbid, but if anything happened to us, I'd like to think you'd be there to take care of her."

"Seriously, Sally? Wow. Why is it that you are always so right about everything? How can I say no? By which I mean, I'd love to be Lowen's Guardian. And I'd love to be your friend. And yes, I'd love to get to know Simon again too. We had been good friends once and there is no reason why we can't be again."

"Phew. That went better than I thought. Brace yourself now, because I'm going to knock you off your seat with my belly whilst I try to hug you. Sorry – I've got hormones – I think I'm going to cry."

After reluctantly separating himself from Sally's hug, Matthew's analytical mind kicked back into action.

"What do you mean? 'Better than planned'."

"Yes, I told you, Simon and I discussed it. We are in total agreement."

"Yes, you said. But 'planned'?"

"Ah, I see what you mean. How did I know where to find you to ask you?"

"Yes. Oh - I was on that bench on that green on the first day of the month. You knew, didn't you? You knew I'd be there. You came to meet me, didn't you?"

"Maybe."

"How? How did you know? What do you mean, *maybe*?"

"Allow a girl a few secrets, Matthew. Let's just say that you are a creature of habit."

"Why do I think there is more to it?"

"Because there is. Because you are too smart for your own good. But that's all you are getting. Let's order."

Their coffees and their conversation mellowed in the comforting café culture that they shared. Talk of separate and linked futures reconciled their disparateness and affection laced with overtones of a lost love nursed their comity. Having agreed to meet again and to nurture their friendship, they embraced and parted each to their respective lives. Sally to her partner and her impending parturition and Matthew to his empty house overlooking the River Cam.

Unable to focus on preparation for the start of a next term Matthew opened his laptop and stared at the nearly completed text for his new book. No chapter formed in his mind. No words fell from his fingers. He had reached an impasse. He felt that he had reached the end of a journey but did not know where he had arrived and nor had he planned a new one.

Another January

On the first day of the first month of another new year Matthew strolled circumspectly towards that bench on that green. The sky had broken into a jigsaw of grey clouds and white candyfloss together with a crisp azure which beckoned winter to abate. It was mid-morning and the excesses of the previous night had left him tired but otherwise clear-headed.

Christmas, for once, had been a highlight. His parents had not only unconditionally accepted that their traditional Christmas dinner would be abandoned, but, to Matthew's astonishment, they and his sister had joined him in Cambridge to serve dinners to homeless souls in the crypt of St Mary's Church. Matthew had joined Michelle at her table and had engaged in sombre but uplifting conversations as tales of homeless life were shared along with paper hats and turkey legs. Perhaps the most astonishing development for Matthew was that, as he absorbed the stories unfolding in the crypt, he had had no intention of analysing them nor of quoting them in his next book. Instead, he found genuine engagement, empathy and connection. He also found himself capable of casual and agreeable conversation without the need for critical interrogation.

The New Year's Eve party, however, had been a low point. It had been, by any standards, a successful party. The same people as last year had exchanged the same conversations as last year. The same people that Matthew knew were there as they were each year. But something had changed. Matthew had changed, but as yet, he did not recognise the transition that he had undergone and which was now unsettling him. Eva had made an appearance complete with her new baby and, well before midnight, Matthew had walked her back to her new apartment and had sat with her until the New Year broke their discourse. In the newly emerging minutes of the new year, and after sharing the kiss that friends are able to share without complexity, he had left her and made his way back to his house overlooking Jesus Green pleased that this new year had seen the beginnings of a newly formed Matthew.

His gait was casual and reflective that morning on Jesus Green but, as that bench came into view, he saw a diminutive but pretty woman sitting staring into the distance. He felt she had a tale to tell. He felt that her presence was drawing him into her world. Without the need for further self-interrogation, he maintained his contemplative stride, fixed his stare ahead and walked past. *"No more,"* he thought. *"No more holding time back sitting on that bench. No more. Goodbye, dear bench. There is a future out there somewhere and it is not to be found on that bench."*

Matthew allowed himself one final indulgence. He had one more farewell to make before directing his life in a way in which he now felt compelled to do albeit in a direction he had yet to discover. He retraced his steps of the previous year. Precisely one year ago, he had met Heidi. He and Heidi had found a bond that had propelled him on a yearlong journey.

He had to lay the memory of Heidi to rest before he could move on.

He retraced his steps, one stride at a time, along the path and over the bridge to the ArtTime Gallery where he paused to take in the image that he had held in his mind on the first day of each of the twelve months that had passed. He imagined himself with Heidi. He imagined how he might have been able to hold on to her long enough to form a lasting bond. He rehearsed words in his head which would have captivated her and persuaded her to be part of his life. But these were just imaginings. He had to say goodbye to Heidi. He had to lay her memory to rest. *"If only,"* he pondered. Then, barely aware that his thoughts had found an audible voice, "Oh, Heidi. Heidi. Goodbye. If only."

"Yes?" Came an ethereal response.

Not sure if the voice was real or imagined, Matthew slowly turned and stared. His stare was met with a broad smile from a vision of Heidi. Matthew became statuesque as he slowly scanned the vision and began deconstructing his disbelief. Her mousy hair which was neither straight nor curly still adorned a head sitting atop a brightly coloured scarf. The navy-blue duffle coat which he had imagined month after month had been replaced by a camel jacket and the drab brown trousers had been replaced by faded, purple corduroys. Flat, leather shoes still completed the picture. There may have been cosmetic differences between the reality before him and his memory, but the overpowering image was unmistakably Heidi.

"Hello Matthew. Good to see you at last?"

"But …"

"Try not to think too hard for a moment. I don't want to spoil this moment."

"But …"

"Well, don't I get a hug?"

"Christ, Heidi. It's so nice to see you. But …"

"Can we get past the 'but' stage, please? Look, I've outguessed you – see what I've got here? I've got two takeaway coffees from the Café Cam. Fancy a stroll along the Cam?"

"Coffee? Stroll? Yes. But …"

"And, maybe when you've recovered your powers of speech, we might even have a conversation. What do you think? Up for it? I think I might have a bit of explaining to do."

"But …"

Coffee and ambulation engaged their unity until Matthew was finally able to ask the question that he had asked himself on each of the first days on each of the months whilst sitting on that bench on that green.

"Heidi. We had a date on the first day of February. We agreed to meet at the bench. We agreed to meet at lunchtime. I went there as promised. You didn't show."

"Well, Matthew. Actually, I did."

"But I was there. You weren't."

"I know. I saw you."

"What? But why didn't you come over? I waited for you."

"I saw you, Matthew. I saw you with another woman. I waited, but you seemed to be with her. She was on a mobility scooter. Then you went off with her."

"But …"

"But I didn't want to intrude. The truth is, I went to watch at that bench on the first day of every month. Every month I saw you with another woman. Every month you went off with another woman. So, I waited."

"Heidi. I never knew. This is terrible. I promise you I wasn't *going off* with these women. They were just chance encounters."

"Well, I saw you with each and every one of them. The one with the dog for instance. Oh, and that teenage sex-kitten with spray-on lycra. You'll have to forgive me for hating her just a little bit. I don't know how it is even possible to exist with a body like that. She clearly wanted to be naked."

"Kayla. That was Kayla. She was a student. I promise you, none of them was a date and I didn't go off with any of them. Especially Kayla."

"I know. It's alright, you don't have to explain. It's just, well, it's just that any one of those encounters could have ended in a date. Don't pretend otherwise. You were looking, weren't you? But, just put yourself in my shoes. How could I have come over when you were with someone else? Anyway, today I was there too. Today, you walked past that bench. Today you went to the gallery. So today, I met you."

"But …"

"But I had to be sure. I had to wait. I wanted to be sure you actually wanted me. I needed to know that you were ready. I've been pissed around too many times to take chances."

"I am ready, Heidi. None of those women were for me. It was you. I went there every month hoping to see you."

"OK, Matthew. Do you reckon we might have a proper date, or something?"

"Oh, God, yes. Yes please. Please let's go on a date. A real date. Does that make me sound a bit desperate?"

"A bit. Well, anyway Matthew, I'm a bit of catch, actually. Some might even describe me as being *good looking, nice tits, fairly smart.*"

"Huh? But ..."

"Come on Matthew, get that brilliant mind of yours into gear. With a little effort you'll get there. *Good looking, nice tits, fairly smart.* Ring any bells?"

"But that's what Sally said. She wanted to hook me up with a friend of hers who she described as *good looking, nice tits, fairly smart.*"

"Nearly there, Matthew. One final push. Try to put it together."

"So, you are Sally's friend? You know Sally? You are friends with Sally? Sally was trying to set me up with you? That's how Sally knew where to find me – you told her. Why the hell didn't Sally say who it was?"

"Phew. At last. Well done. Yes, I've known Sally for a year now. I first met her at the New Year's Eve party a year ago. Remember, the party I said I nearly hooked up with a guy. Well, that came to nothing, but I ended up with a new girly friend? Well, it turns out my new girly friend was your ex. Sally and I hit it off and just stayed friends. She is really nice. Next time I saw her I told her about this guy I'd met on Jesus Green and, well, between us, we worked out that it was you.

It took us a while to make the connection. Anyway, she's been trying to set me up with different guys all year, but she's always known I've had a thing for you. I made her promise not to say anything. I needed to do this all by myself."

"Oh, my God. My poor brain. I can't cope. Give me an academic treatise to unravel and I'll crack it in no time, but I can't cope with all this."

"Do you want to know something else?"

"Go on. Nothing you could say can shock me now."

"You know Sally is about to bring baby Lowen into the world?"

"Yes. I met with her — which I bet you already know. And she asked me to be a Guardian — which I bet you already know."

"Yes. I already knew. Well, anyway, they've planned the Christening and, well, we will be Godparents together."

"What? You are kidding me."

"Yes. You and me. Oh, I mean Guardians. I thought Guardians was a good idea too. We'll be Lowen's Guardians together. Matthew and Heidi — Guardians to baby Lowen."

"Wow. OK, now my mind has blown. Just amazing. Brilliant. But frankly, I'm feeling a bit dizzy trying to catch up with you. You are light years ahead of me."

"Sorry. I feel I've ambushed you a bit. Anyway, Matthew, now that you are getting your powers of speech back, I hear you have some big news of your own. Professorship. Sally tells me you have got it in the bag. Right?"

"Well, yes. The Academic Board meets in a month. Word is they will grant me professorship at last."

"Why so glum. Isn't that what you've been working yourself to a frazzle for, for the past year?"

"Well, yes, but I'm not sure I want it now. I might just be having second thoughts now it's going to happen."

"How come? It's what you've always wanted, isn't it? It's a real honour."

"It is, but now it's happening it feels like a bear trap. If I become a professor, there will be no escape. My life will never change. I'll forever be trapped in an academic world doing professorial things. They will own me and own every word that comes out of me. I'm not sure I could stand a whole life just doing that. My eyes have been opened a bit this last year and I sort of want something new. I just feel very different about my life now. The problem is, I just don't know what I want. The truth is, I've realised that no matter how smart I appear to be, I'm actually very dumb. I'm really blinkered. I graduated at Cambridge, I got a master's at Cambridge and I got a Doctorate at Cambridge. I lecture at Cambridge and soon I'll be owned by Cambridge. I will call myself Professor of Anthropology but now I've learned that I know nothing about life and even less about myself."

"I'm feeling a bit the same too if I'm honest. I'm not sure I want to be a primary school teacher all my life. I do still enjoy teaching, but I don't want promotion and I'm sick to the back teeth of Ofsted breathing down my neck and I'm sick of crap teachers who got promoted out of the classroom thinking they know better than me. The final straw has been a new Teaching Assistant I've been given, called Judith. She's one of the ones you met at your bench. She's a nightmare. Anyway, I want to find something more creative. Something that lets me do new stuff rather than just keep churning out the same old curriculum using the same old resources. I feel like a robot on a conveyer belt. I wonder if there is something else in me. So, anyway, what are your options?"

"I genuinely don't know. But, do you remember when we first met, I told you that I was going to Cape Town?"

"I remember very well. We did the exhibition in the gallery and you told me you had a trip planned. I was very jealous. I so wanted to go with you. How did it go?"

"It went exceptionally well."

"I'd love to hear about it."

"I'd love to tell you all about it. Do you know what the best thing about the trip was?"

"What?"

"Well, on my first trip to Khayelitsha I stayed in a five-star hotel. This time I actually stayed in Khayelitsha itself. It kind of shocked my college. I think they thought I'd get murdered. I stayed at Vicky's bed and breakfast. Right in the heart of Khayelitsha."

"Wow. I'm jealous all over again."

"It was brilliant. It used to boast that it was the smallest B and B in the world, but I don't know if that's true. It is definitely tiny. Just one bedroom. But Vicky was lovely. She's like everyone's favourite mum."

"I so want to go and stay there."

"Yeah, you should. I spent my entire time there. Living in Khayelitsha and living with the people. I ate with them and drank with them and talked with them. I spent most evenings in the shebeens just talking and laughing. My students were scared stiff."

"Shebeens?"

"Shebeens are like pubs. A bar, some tables and usually a tv with football on it. Shebeens are a real social centre. You know, they were so kind to me. They just accepted me for who I was. They are so poor, but never once begged from me. They shared whatever they had with me. Another thing you might be interested in as a primary school teacher is that, despite having no money, the school kids wear school uniform. They are immaculately turned out. They take a real pride in their uniforms and in their schools. The school kids just want to learn."

"Just stop, Matthew. I have to go. I will go. I will."

"Yeah, you must. Did you know that their proudest boast is that, although they are poor, no-one ever goes hungry in Khayelitsha because whoever has food always shares it? They mostly cook in the streets and anyone who needs food is welcome to call by and join in."

"That's it, I'm booking to go."

"Just do it. Maybe I could be your guide. I learned so much from those people. I think I finally understood the meaning of ubuntu. I knew so much about ubuntu from just about every angle, but I never actually understood it. I learned more in two weeks than any book or lecture or seminar ever taught me."

"Ubuntu?"

"Ubuntu – let's save that for a conversation over dinner, Heidi."

"OK. Dinner? That's a definite date then."

"Definitely. I'm not letting you go this time. Anyway, the University of Cape Town actually offered me a yearlong contract as a visiting lecturer if I wanted it. The plan would have been to research teaching and learning strategies in Khayelitsha with a view to setting up a new curriculum. Primary school stuff initially but then secondary school too. It would have informed a new education policy. The pay would have been crap, but the work would have been amazing. I really think I could have achieved something. Something really important. Something real. Something I could be proud of."

"And did you turn it down?"

"I said I'd think about it and they said they'd leave the offer open for as long as it took me to decide."

"Still thinking? What's stopping you? How about following your heart?"

"I'm not sure what's stopping me. The professorship thing, I guess. I've worked so hard to get it. It's a once in a lifetime opportunity. I'd be mad to turn it down."

"But you are having doubts?"

"Yes, but meeting you has made my mind up. If we are going to date, then I'm staying. Do you fancy dinner with a nearly-professor?"

"Not wanting to be mean or anything, Matthew, but I'm not actually impressed by the professorship thing. I know it will be a great achievement and you should be very proud of yourself. I'll be very proud of you. But I'd rather date an actual person than a professor."

"I take your point. That's exactly it. I want to be me not a professor. Why is everyone so much cleverer than me? You see, Heidi this is just the sort of thing I was talking about. I have met lots of different people this year and they have all talked sense to me. Even when I didn't like what they said. It's made me re-evaluate everything. You are one hundred percent right. Being a person is more important than being a professor."

"Maybe you should take it. Take the visiting lectureship thingy. Go to Cape Town and be the person you want to be. Do what you want to. Do it for yourself."

"Maybe you are right. Wise words. So, Heidi. I have some wise words for you in return. You say you are at a career crossroads too. You told me you really fancied going to Cape Town and maybe teaching in Khayelitsha. Well, if I accept the visiting lecturer post, then come with me. Let's do it together."

"But ..."

"Who's 'butting' now?

"Are you serious Matthew?"

"I am one hundred percent serious. Let's take a year out together and follow our hearts."

"How would it work?"

"I dunno. We'd have to work it out together. I guess we'd both resign our jobs. I'd take up the visiting lecturer post for a year and you'd teach in the charity school. We'd get ourselves an apartment and, well, and then we'd work it out as we went along."

"Maybe. To be honest, I can't think of anything I'd rather do. And, standby to cringe, but I can't think of anyone I'd rather do it with. But shall we at least have a first date before running off to the other side of the world together?"

"Well. Maybe we've already had loads of dates. On the first day of every month since we first met."

"You weirdo, Matthew. They were only nearly-dates."

"What do you say, Heidi? I'm up for it if you are. Say yes."

"Yes."

Cover art by Pam Cotgreave
https://www.instagram.com/dovepotterycornwall

Portraits by Matthew Taylor

Printed in Great Britain
by Amazon